To Begin Again

Jen Knox

ALL THINGS

THAT MATTER

PRESS

To Begin Again

ISBN 13: 9780984629787

Library of Congress Control Number: 2011902203

Cover design by All Things That Matter Press
Cover graphics by *Laura J. Miller*
Published in 2011 by All Things That Matter Press

This collection is dedicated to my sister, Laura Knox.

Acknowledgments

"Always a Story" was originally published in slightly different form as a Reader's Narrative in *Narrative Magazine*. "At the Window" originally appeared in *Annalemma Magazine*. "Disengaged" was published in *Superstition Review* and was later chosen for publication as Short Story of the Week in *Short Story America*. "The Probability of Him" was first published in *Eclectic Flash*; "D20-Xc8" and "Negligence" were first published in *San Antonio Current*. And in slightly different forms, "Dandelion Ghosts" was first published in *Bananafish*, "Levity" was introduced in *Metazen*, and "To the Curb" in *Midwest Literary Magazine*. "A Little Taste of Heaven" first appeared in *Bartleby Snopes* and received Story of the Month for January, 2011; "Cheers" has appeared in *The Bennington Review*. "Soft like Snow" was originally published in *Foundling Review*.

At the Window

It felt more like an accident, as though I struck his fist with my mouth. But the man who punched me loosened two of my front bottom teeth and introduced me to a common social phenomenon that he had, no doubt, defined for himself long before.

I had money on me, not a lot but enough to qualify me as a decent mark had the man wanted to rob me. Had he robbed me, I would have had the simple luxury of anger toward him. As it happened, however, he didn't want a thing from me. He barely glanced in my direction—just planted a cross-hook to my lip and continued to walk as though he hadn't seen me at all.

He looked to be in his forties. His skin was sun-beaten and he walked slowly. Much like many of the men I saw walking down Front Street in worn clothes and with matted hair, his gaze was cast down toward his feet. I thought little of the fact that he was talking to himself, but because he was the only person nearby, and because he didn't seem to notice me, I had been staring at him as we moved toward each other.

I didn't hear every word, but one would become clear. He said it three times: "Bitch. Fucking bitch. You fucking bitch," as his knuckles collided with my chin and lips. Our eyes met briefly before he continued his conversation and walked on.

I stood there stunned a moment before I began to scream. I let out wails so loud that they shocked even me. I yelled out for someone to help, thinking no one could hear when I began to notice them one by one, the people who were watching, surrounding me. Dozens of faces in office and car windows.

It was a warm day and around lunch hour. My mouth was numb, my stomach burned with panic. When I realized no one was going to offer help, I ran toward a man at the end of the block, who tried to avoid the situation by hurrying away.

"Please," I yelled, "call the police."

As he dialed, he shuffled his feet. As he spoke, he straightened his tie. He didn't offer me the phone or ask me questions about what happened.

After the police were called, the man told me everything would be fine, help was coming, and he walked away.

I was alone again, on a busy street. I tried to meet eyes with as many people as I could: so many of them still there with blank expressions, all watching the girl who had been screaming, covered in blood. Anger welled up inside me as I sat down to wait.

***

Years later, as a college student, I was introduced to Genovese Syndrome in a social psychology course that I took every Thursday night. "The syndrome," Professor Wilbur explained, "was coined after the 1964 murder of a young woman named Kitty Genovese." He read from a newspaper article. It reported that more than a dozen people eye-witnessed the attack. Each of these witnesses—her neighbors—had heard Kitty's screams for help and watched as she was brutalized. What was most disturbing about this case, as far as our class was concerned, wasn't the number of eyewitnesses, but the fact that none of them went to Kitty's aid, even after she was stabbed twice in the back. He finished the story.

"After the stabbing, Kitty lay in her apartment hallway for nearly ten minutes until the same man who stabbed her returned and raped her. A couple minutes after this second attack, a neighbor finally called the police, but by this time it was too late. Kitty died before she reached the hospital."

I stayed up that night, poring over the assigned reading and then every article I could find online about the case and the psychological theories for the apathy these neighbors seemed to exhibit.

The Kitty Genovese Syndrome, otherwise known as Bystander Syndrome, offers little more than a phrase for a disturbing pattern in human behavior: *As the number of eye-witnesses increases, the chance that any one person from the group intervenes decreases.* Knowing that psychology has defined a phenomenon I witnessed meant that I hadn't been singled out. I was no longer alone. I was merely on the receiving end of a predictable reaction to negative stimuli. But when I set out to write a paper on the subject, I came to a disturbing question. What if I had been one of Kitty Genovese's neighbors, woken by her screams in the night, stunned by the scene of her slow and torturous murder? I requested another topic for my paper on social psychology and, after the course was complete, I found myself less consumed by the topic.

It's been over a decade since the blow, and after root canals, my teeth have been salvaged. I no longer feel disgust toward those people who watched me from their windows, but when I do think of that day, I sometimes wonder whether one of those people, just one, would have intervened if the attack had been more severe. What if the man had been multiple men? What if the man stabbed me? What if he had continued to strike until I stopped moving? What if I had not been the victim but a witness?

When a police officer arrived, I ran up to him and told him my story, quickly so as not to waste any more time. I pointed, said, "He went that way. I bet you can find him. He just walked, he didn't run." Instead of the policeman running after the offender, he asked me to calm down and describe the man. Then he asked me if I knew the assailant. When I said no, he asked me again. "Are you sure this isn't a domestic dispute?"

"No," I yelled. "There was something wrong with him. I think he was crazy, probably homeless. He looked homeless."

The officer nodded knowingly. "We've had a few of these cases since a facility was shut down a few blocks away. Quite a few of those guys have turned up on the streets. I hate to say it, Miss, but even if we do catch this guy, he'll probably just spend a night in jail. He'll probably be thankful for a warm bed, but we won't be able to keep him long." He said it all in a reassuring voice, but his each word seemed to further deflate my expectation that someone, anyone, would try to help.

***

I don't think he saw me, even when our eyes met. He just happened to pull back and swing, happened to place a blow just as we passed each other, and I happened to be on the receiving end. I happened to be there during the height of his anger, and I happened to be a target—wrong place, wrong time. I never felt anger toward this man. It was all so painless at the time. In fact, I felt nothing at all until my tongue found the space where my teeth used to be and I began to feel the warmth of blood rushing down my chin and neck. It was, to my mind, more an act of nature than one of aggression, or even free will. In a strange way, in fact, I feel as though he were as much a victim of his own rage as I had been. So why not extend the same sympathies to the people in the window? To the pessimistic officer? They were, after all, just acting in accord to a predictable response. They felt no responsibility—or maybe the responsibility was spread too thin.

In the moments after my attack, in the depth of self-pity, I believed that no one came to my aid because I, personally, wasn't worthy of it. Years later, while I studied the psychological theory that was put in place to explain such apathetic behavior, I felt an odd sense of relief.

I realize now that most people remain at the window from time to time, desensitized by their distance from a problem. We all watch collectively as acts of sickness and even depravity occur, if only it's far enough away. On some level, I imagine the man who punched me has felt he is on the receiving end of the Genovese Syndrome each time a girl walks past him on his way to work.

***

I teach English at a community college. It was here that a student, Eric, asked if I could take a look at a research paper he was writing for a sociology course. The thesis of his paper went something like this: Crimes are easier to commit if you spend time with criminals. He was having trouble citing a news story that recounted a recent attack in Richmond. A fifteen year old girl had been on her way home from school when a group of teenage boys asked her if she wanted to hang out, get some drinks. She went. By the end of the night, the girl had been gang-raped and beaten by seven boys while numerous other teenagers watched, but did not intervene. Eric clapped his hands, said, "The girl should've known better than to hang out with a large group of teenage boys she barely knew." I asked him how he felt about the boys who had brutalized this girl. "It was wrong and they were horrible, but there are bad people in the world, and this girl should've known better," he said with resolve. I asked him what he thought of the other teenagers who witnessed this brutality and didn't act. "They were aiding and abetting." I pressed my tongue to my bottom teeth.

The story included interviews from those who witnessed the crime, but hadn't intervened for various reasons. None of the attackers had a voice in the piece. I suggested the student consider changing his thesis to attempt to explain the onlookers' behavior and, this way, he could cite their interviews.

"That's great," he said. "I can still use all the same notes. It's virtually the same topic." He left with a strong thesis, he said, and a clear head. Later in the week when I saw the student again, I asked him how the last essay had turned out. He said he'd thought about it for a long time after our meeting and, although I helped him a lot, he decided to cite a different news story, to choose a different subject.

I wanted to say he couldn't do that, he had to stick with the topic, our topic.

"Flush it out, raise awareness, push boundaries," I wanted to yell. Instead of repeating my frenzied thoughts, however, I said, "I understand." But my words came out in a wounded tenor. Eric smiled brightly, as though he was heartened by my investment in his work. And, as if to assure me, he said he'd saved the paper and still planned to finish it one day, when he was ready.

Eric has moved on, transferred to another school, and I have yet to see his paper realized. For some reason, I can't shake my disappointment about this, nor can I ignore the irrationality of my disappointment. After all, as an undergraduate student myself, I had been blocked on the same idea.

Perhaps it was because the topic was too big or too close, but more than likely I just didn't want to think about it. I didn't want to research a subject that would make me question a tendency that I knew, gutturally, I was not exempt from. If I was exempt, after all, I would have the luxury of anger toward the man who hit me, and the right to move on. I would be able to have nightmares about that day without seeing my own face behind glass, without waking up to ask who I've watched from my window. And addressing this simple question changes everything.

Like Smoke

Amira stood at the center of a circular display in a store near Gate 33B. Ordinarily, she felt tranquil among the constant, hurried motion of travelers. Today, however, a self-conscious, restlessness overtook her as she paced the sales floor between customers, rehearsing her request. The manager, Irene, was in her closet-sized office, as usual and, as usual, she had announced her plans to leave after she counted the deposits, which meant there wasn't much time.

Since Amira's father died, she watched her savings account dwindle as daily living expenses soared. She couldn't afford to work only part-time anymore. Roy had told his daughter that she'd never have to worry; he had a few investments he wanted her to inherit. But, because Gloria, her mother, was listed as the executor of his estate when he died—and there was no one less deserving, if you asked Amira—she knew she'd never see a penny. Since Amira's early childhood, her mother had maintained a ghostlike presence in her daughter's life, only visible in pictures and dreams; only heard late at night, slurring and incomprehensible through a drunken stupor, or a sentimental call.

After Roy's funeral, Gloria announced her plans to leave right away. "It'd just be too painful to stay," she'd said, her tone and manner unconvincing. She turned to Amira for a brief semi-maternal moment, brushed a thick dark curl from her daughter's face, placed a skinny tanned arm around the girl's shoulder and said, "This is hard, but you're eighteen now. You have to learn to take care of yourself."

And that was it. Gloria's tone shifted then as she lit a cigarette and announced her plans to audition for a new reality TV show that followed the lives of female truckers—in which she would play the antagonistic, outspoken role in hopes of getting her own show one day. A few days later, she was gone, leaving only traces of smoke and patchouli, behind. She hadn't shed a tear.

***

"If anyone can handle a tough spot, it's you, kiddo," Roy used to tell his daughter. But here she was now, a year after his death, a month away from eviction if she didn't come up with some money soon. Handling the situation seemed an abstract concept.

There was so much riding on Irene's answer that the question itself seemed to take on a weight that settled at the base of Amira's throat. She spent many hours thinking of the proper way to phrase her request to avoid sounding desperate. "I am ready to start working full-time," she rehearsed in a voice she thought sounded confident, entitled even. It was a voice she heard from the most frequent travelers, those who knew the most efficient and unencumbered ways to travel, who could afford the small perks that came with big fees, one of which was a ten percent discount at this store. A customer, who had been reading a magazine for the past twenty minutes, decided to approach her just then. He shuffled toward the counter and handed her a pack of gum, which she quickly rang up.

"Two dollars? What are you guys doing to me here?" he asked. He wore a fedora and a threadbare brown suit that Amira thought to be at least ten years old. She gave him a sympathetic shrug. "I could understand raising prices a little for convenience, but this is robbery. It's indecent," he went on.

"Sorry. But I don't make the prices."

He sneered, sighed, did everything inaudible a person can do to portray irritation, and placed a fifty dollar bill on the counter. Amira wondered why a person who cared enough to complain would go ahead and break a fifty for something that cost two dollars. She counted out his change and placed it on the counter avoiding contact with the man. Two more people got in line.

"Where can I smoke?" a young woman asked. She was around Amira's age, with straight black hair parted at the side in an unflattering diagonal line across her pale forehead. Amira told her that the only place to smoke was in the lounge in Gate D on the other side of the airport, to which the girl answered "Shit" and then tucked her bangs behind her ear. "Are you sure that's the nearest lounge? Figures. I won't make it. My plane leaves in twenty minutes."

"The smoking area is pretty gross anyway," Amira said.

8

"Yeah. Well, thanks. You all are out of the small bottled waters over there. I didn't want to buy the big one." Two more customers got in line.

"I can get you a small one," Amira offered. The waters were in Irene's office, and they were warm, but the store was beginning to fill with travelers and this might be the only opportunity Amira would have to let Irene know that she had to talk with her. The girl began to protest, and Amira added, "No trouble. Just one second."

She knocked on the door and when the metal handle turned, all her insecurities returned and reduced her voice, making it small and shaky as she said, "Hi, Irene. Um, we're busy right now, but I wanted to catch you before you leave today. Do you think we can talk?"

"Is it important? I was just getting ready to leave. I have a volleyball tournament tonight." Amira looked past her, to Irene's Twitter page.

"It's about the schedule. Um…" Irene clicked something on her screen to pull up a spreadsheet then swiveled around in her chair and stared up at Amira impatiently. Irene was a tall woman and her long graceful legs were crossed in a meditative position that seemed a stark contrast to her impatient glare. She ground her square jaw rapidly, chewing gum that Amira was sure hadn't cost two dollars, or if it had, it wouldn't have been a big deal. Management made good money. "I wanted to know if there was a full-time position available." Maybe this was too pushy. After all, any hours would help and Amira needed what she could get. "You know, since Randy left, I thought some hours might be available."

There were three people in line behind the smoker and all of them were watching Amira wilt in front of her boss while they commiserated about their delayed flights or those they had to catch right now. Irene, who almost never smiled, bit the end of her pen, causing her mouth to curl up at the edges. This was a woman who had begun locking the office door when Amira entered one day without knocking and interrupted some kind of chanting session Irene had been reciting.

"Can't you see I'm centering myself? Fuck, Amira, knock," she'd yelled. "Tell you what," Irene said, removing the pen from her mouth. "We'll discuss this later, but I'll be completely honest, I don't know if we have the hours." She looked up at the screen that surveyed her store and motioned toward it. "I see you have a bunch of customers out there waiting, and I'll be leaving soon, so now probably isn't the best time. Do me a favor and drop those envelopes in the safe for me and get back out there. We'll discuss this later."

As Amira turned toward the safe, there was a loud pang, followed by the unmistakable sound of yet another customer knocking over the rack of neck pillows and T-shirts. Irene's eyes darted toward the camera and before Amira could move out of the way, she was up and pushing out the door to make sure the customer was putting the display back together, which, surprisingly, he was.

Returning to her station, Amira realized she had forgotten the water. She didn't want to return to the office, she couldn't, and so she told the girl that she was sorry they were out, after all. "I was going to buy the big one anyway," the girl said, pulling a twenty from a coin purse that was attached to the belt loop of her jeans. When Amira placed the bill in the register, she noticed that the gentleman's fifty dollar bill was gone. She searched around the drawer, trying to look nonchalant about the loss, but realized that she had no memory of actually putting the bill in the drawer. She looked underneath the till, then under the twenties, where she would sometimes place larger bills. Had he scammed her or had the bill simply dropped somewhere? She couldn't look suspicious on the video, so she shut the register and greeted the next customer.

A few more people bought a few more things, and each time Amira opened the drawer, she reexamined it as though convinced she'd just missed it the last time she looked. She couldn't remember anything after he handed to her, only her own nervousness about speaking with Irene. Now, she thought, Irene will probably think I stole that fifty, and it'll be even harder to convince her otherwise, now that I asked for more hours. She'll think I'm desperate for money, she'll think I'm running some kind of scam, trying to gain her sympathy so that she might forgive me and we can partner in a mutually agreeable don't ask, don't tell. Amira's imagination began to spiral toward the worst case scenario. She imagined the irritation in Irene's voice when she called in the morning after the drawer turns up short; how Irene will yell about having to open the safe and count the deposits, each one, along with the credit receipts. Amira had to find that fifty.

Irene hustled out the door twenty minutes before closing, not saying goodbye or we'll talk later about your request, or anything else to Amira before leaving. She was met by an equally large, athletic woman and they hugged and laughed as their size ten heels clacked against linoleum. Amira felt a small wave of relief as she watched them go. It was almost time to close down the store and she was eager to get home. The barrage of customers all day had been a mere backdrop to her shifting but well-fed anxiety, and she felt physically drained. She remembered that she had to pick up seed for her parakeet and toilet paper.

As she counted down the drawer at the end of the night and signed her initials to the paper taped to its side, she had calmed down, remembering that could find a new job. Her father had a good friend named Craig who managed the Pancake House a mile from her apartment. It didn't pay as well, and the work was grueling, but she'd always have a job; he'd always have a waitress on the verge of quitting. Craig had placed a hand on the small of her back a few days after her father's funeral when he and his wife had stopped by to drop off a casserole. She'd thanked him, felt his fingers working their way down, and pulled away sharply. He didn't flinch; his wife, whose eyes had been on her husband's hand, seemed oddly bemused.

A few days before her father lost control of his truck on the way home from work, he said to her, "You always bounce back, Mira. And remember, I'm doing all the suffering for both of us, so you'll never have to go through anything like this. I've paid any karmic debt you can rack up." It was an ominous warning. But Amira thought now that it was his way of owning what would happen to him, of promising he'd always be there, watching out for her.

Imagining the look on Irene's face as she counted the drawer the next morning, Amira actually began to chuckle. Maybe the fifty disappeared just to put things into perspective. She knew better than to think she'd ever really get full-time status.

"Fuck this place," she said, turning off the lights. And just as she was locking up, the man in the fedora approached her. "Ma'am, ma'am, you need to open that place back up now," he said.

"Sorry, sir, but we're closed. I can't open it back up. The alarm will go off."

"But you gave me my fifty back in my change."

"Well I can't go back in there." Amira said.

"I don't care. I just don't want any trouble. You'd rather I give it to a security guard?"

Amira considered the few security guards she knew and said, "No, I'll take it. Thank you for your honesty, Sir. I'll return it in the morning"

"Pay better attention, young lady," he said, shuffling away, and she wondered what ailment kept him from picking up his feet.

The fifty was crisp, almost brittle, but she knew two minutes in the Florida heat would moisten it, give it some wear. She rolled it up and slid it into her back pocket. Amira dialed the work number from her cell, to leave a message. "Hello, um, it's Amira. I am calling to let the opener know that the drawer should be exactly fifty dollars short in the morning, but that the customer who short changed me fessed up and brought back the bill. I'll bring it in first thing. It was just a mix-up." She felt as though she was rambling, sounding nervous, dishonest even, and she pressed the pound key, hoping the machine would give her another chance. A recording instructed her to press seven if she'd like to erase and rerecord, which she did. The seven key seemed to stick, though, and a beep came through the line followed by, "If you'd like to erase your message and rerecord..." and then another beep, which set off the same cycle of automated prompts. She shut off the phone and took the bus to the grocery store.

Amira used the fifty to pay for her parakeet's food and the toilet paper, but this would only mean a trip to the bank on the way to work tomorrow, no biggie. Then again, if she were to go in the morning, before the airport stores began to open, the banks wouldn't be operating yet, and she wasn't sure she could get that much out of an ATM. This would keep Irene from digging out the week's deposits. "Sometimes you just have to listen to the universe," Roy used to say. But what the hell was it trying to tell her with this series of events? She considered returning the items she'd purchased and asking for the same fifty dollar bill in return, but instead she continued to walk; it was easier to just go home. Besides, she imagined the bird was hungry and it'd be cruel to make him wait.

When Amira arrived home, Roy greeted her with a loud screeching noise then began to bob his head madly. She opened his cage and let him fly around a bit to calm down. It always gave her a good feeling to watch him fly. Outside of eating, it seemed his only pleasure. 'Roy the bird' was named after Amira's father. He was a namesake, and something about that fact, the fact that her father had given his bird his own name, seemed now too like a sign from her father. As long as the bird was there, he'd be watching over her. She wiped down her phone and dialed Craig's number to ask him if the waitressing position was still available. He said of course it was; when did she want to start? "I have a uniform all ready for you, a small right?" His voice dripped with the promise of sexual harassment. She opened the window, allowing a soft breeze to enter. Roy flew to the sill.

"I'll call you back, Craig. Thanks."

Amira filled Roy's dish with seed. She watched the small blue bird peck away behind his cage, the cage that kept him from his curiosity. She decided to leave the door open for him, just in case he changed his mind. She looked at her phone, thinking that it might be a good move to call the store again and leave a message, explaining that the cash drawer would be a little short, but there was no reason to panic. She rehearsed her message, then decided it would be better to call in the morning, then decided she wouldn't call at all. Instead, she dialed the number of the airport directory. And as she paced the floor, on hold for an inordinate amount of time, she heard the squak, the flutter of wings, and turned around just in time to see Roy take off.

Irene left a message the next morning at the apartment. She began her message by saying "It's a Federal offense to steal money from the workplace, and we will prosecute to the full extent of the law. We found the drawer fifty dollars short this morning, and I went to count the deposits... Where are the deposits, Amira? I'm giving you an opportunity here, Amira, to call me back and confess. If you return the money, we might be able to work something out." The message fell on deaf ears, since no one was around to hear it.

The fifty Amira had handed to the customer by mistake had really made her decision easier. It had to be a sign, she knew, that she had to act fast or not at all; she had let the universe decide. Yesterday, as Amira stood in the doorway of Irene's office, asking for more hours like a child desperate for a second cookie, she paused as she held the thin envelopes of freshly counted money, envelopes that were already dated and signed, that wouldn't be looked at again until the guard showed up to collect them late that afternoon. The money, sealed in small manila envelopes, seemed to swell in her hand, swell with opportunity. Amira could be long gone before the deposits were found missing, unless something silly happened, like the cash register came up short. With every eye on the fallen display, she'd been able to stuff the seven envelopes in the front of her pants. It wasn't hard really, thanks to the collapse of a metal display at just the right time. Thanks to her manager's laziness and insistence on leaving early, on denying her a simple request.

Amira hustled toward Gate 16A, on her way to Ohio. There was nothing particularly exciting about Ohio, no one she knew. Further, she imagined things would be tough at first because she'd have to find a job and apartment, a new name; she had no delusions about the reality of landing, the possibility that they would find the missing money and track her ticket before she even landed, but this was for the universe to decide. For now though, as Amira walked, she began to feel her old life falling away from her, and the exhilaration of this—the simple act of walking away—slowed the world around her. She passed the store with only a parting glance, and smiled. She breathed in deep, savoring each step. She boarded the plane, and then, for a short time, the only thing that mattered was the flight.

Soft Like Snow

Elida had the perfect response prepared for this moment, replayed it in her mind so often that she thought it would come automatically. But now that it's here, she's at a loss. Roseanne's skin is cold, rough, and as the sting from the blow works its way from Elida's earlobe to lips, temple to chin, she imagines the hand must share a similar sensation. When the same hand, closed-fist, comes hurling toward her again she ducks just in time. Roseanne's body fumbles forward with the momentum of her own anger, and she falls onto her knee—the bad one—as Elida walks out the front door to the soundtrack of a high, childlike wail.

Although she wears a heavy sweater with sleeves long enough to cover her hands, it is loosely knit and when the wind blows, it bites at the girl's skin. Elida thinks about going back, or maybe she'll go past the bus stop after all, take a left at the bottom of the hill and hole up in the library like she usually does; surround herself with stacks of books, just like the other regulars. Only Elida's titles of choice are not medical books, like the others, but self-improvement or spiritual books: new-agey, pastel colored paperbacks that provide the same advice in a myriad of ways. She thinks about an old, yellowing book she read just last week. It claimed that breath control is a cure-all for any mental or physical ailment. It praised the value of walking meditation, a technique in which a person moves purposefully, taking slow, careful steps, synchronous with the rhythm of his or her breathing.

"Hold your core tight and feel your balance there," her mother used to say, poking her daughter in the stomach. "Once you find it, you can spin forever."

The sky is dark with fat snow-filled clouds that look as though they will never move. Slow steps allow her anger to fall to the ground like the soft snow flakes that were beginning to dot the sky. Elida feels as though she's eight years old again, in her mother's ballet class. Roseanne used to wear her dark hair in a French twist, clap her hands, and a class of small dancers would lift to the balls of their feet. Only Elida would have trouble balancing.

It was during a recital that Roseanne's dancing career eventually ended with a collapse on-stage. Her daughter had watched in horror from the front row as Roseanne's lanky body folded in on itself and the sound of her anguish filled the room. It was the same sound Elida had left behind.

"About face," Roseanne used to instruct with a clap, and the entire group of kids in their pink leotards and tights would spin to face the back of the mirror-lined room.

***

Elida places a shoulder under Roseanne's heavy arm, lifts her up, and smothers her with apologies. She listens as Roseanne cries, prepares toast with honey, gin and tonic. She watches a reality TV show, and joins her mother in laughter when a girl in a skimpy dress says something vulgar, but scripted, about her roommate. Roseanne's breath becomes slower as she sinks into a coma-like slumber. If this were a movie the protagonist would stand over her mother and there would be a soundtrack, ominous or hopeful. Elida glances back at a sickened, bloated body, one that no longer belongs to her mother.

She closes the door behind her. This time, she leaves bundled in a warm, pillow collared down coat, and she knows exactly when the bus will be arriving at the bottom of the snowy hill.

Angelique

The bar's tender, a petite, curvy woman with long hair the color of cinnamon, rolls silverware and ignores customers. Joe notices a purple mark on the inner side of her wrist. He takes a seat and slides his token toward her.

Angelique eyes the token, the man. "What does this look like, an arcade?" She places a half-filled glass in front of him. "When you come up with some money, we can talk about filling this glass."

The Georgia heat creeps in as the front door opens.

"Well, well, well. Look who the hell it is."

Joe closes his fist around the token. "What's the word, Brent?"

"I'm here to find out." A loud, Hawaiian-style button-up shirt accentuates Brent's protruding belly. "Angelique," he calls out, "where you at, girl?"

"Angelique," Joe repeats and laughs.

Brent points toward the token. "You're gold, man, two months?"

Angelique, walking toward Brent with a flirtatious half-smile, a new softness, recaps her lipstick. Her eyes pause briefly on Joe as she passes, checking the space in front of him for cash. Joe is pale from a lack of manual labor, and she believes this means he is delicate. She has no tolerance for brittle men.

"My man gets top-shelf. That chip means he's off court papers," Brent barks.

Angelique musters a crafty smile, imagining the man an inmate. "Congratulations," she says.

Joe notices her smile, revealing a gap in her teeth, which he finds precious.

"Quit talking shit, Angelique. Get that jar out from under the sink. There," Brent instructs.

The clouded jar is labeled Quitters. Angelique carefully places it on a space by the cash register and Joe gets a better look at her wrist. It's a tattoo.

"This is stupid, Brent," she says.

"Fuck you, Angelique, we earned those chips. Those meetings got us off probation; the chips get us free drinks. It's like those customer loyalty cards you use at the grocery store."

Joe stands and flings the chip toward the opening of the jar. It clinks against the side and ricochets. "That's a sign," he says, slightly embarrassed.

Angelique picks up the token, flips it over. She traces the triangle on one side, an emblem of recovery programs. "You sure?" she asks Joe.

"Top-shelf vodka," Brent says, firmly. "I'm not going to drink alone. Hell, that'd make me an alcoholic, right?"

The glass rim against Joe's lip feels natural. The upward tilt and pause and anticipation send flutters into his chest. But Joe never feels the warm bite of vodka on his tongue. His drink is icy instead, shockingly cold and bitter.

Brent's banter becomes less humorous as his eyelids fall. Joe thanks Angelique for the contaminated tap water, but she's busy now and puts her arm up in a sort of frozen wave goodbye. Her thick, smooth arm up, tattooed and still, carves itself in Joe's memory, and he knows he'll be back.

Rationing Sweets

The note I gave the school administrator that morning was not merely an excuse but a detailed storyline, partially adapted from *Days of Our Lives*. The sensitive nature of the material, which included a favorite aunt's chronic illness and severe mental distress on my part, made it nonnegotiable to the authorities. I thought.

Mike and I were upstairs in my room, drinking from small bottles of vodka that a girl at school called "nips" and sold out of her locker between classes. Usually these bottles cost a dollar a piece, but she sold me five for three dollars because, she said, I was one of her best customers. Mike asked if I had a mixer, pineapple juice or some such thing. But, our refrigerator only housed water and milk, and I didn't know where Dad hid the soda—he rationed out sweet things so that we wouldn't over-consume. I told Mike to man up and drink it straight. "Like this," I said, emptying the palm-sized bottle in a few quick gulps.

Mike hooked his finger into the belt loop of my jeans and pulled me close. Our tongues took turns in each other's mouths and I felt my shoulders cave at the tenderness of his lips on my own. This was not the first time I'd kissed a boy, but Mike was different. I enjoyed his touch. He took the time to embrace me and kiss me the way men were supposed to kiss women. He'd brought me a rose that came in a thin plastic tube—it was the first time I'd been given such a gift. I knew that this was becoming serious; we weren't just two kids fooling around.

The high volume on the radio muffled the sounds of the front door opening and my father's keys hitting the table. I didn't hear anything except the monologue in my head telling me that this was it. As Mike's hand went for the button on my jeans, I grabbed his wrist, worry swelling inside me. I was ready for him to get closer, but was I ready for what came after?

The air in my room was viscous and sweet smelling from the perfume I'd sprayed earlier. In anticipation of Mike's arrival, I'd been chain smoking cigarettes that I swiped from my father's stash as I paced the floor of my room nervously, hoping Mike would show up. Mike and I were usually with friends, and the rare moments we'd been alone were spent kissing in a storage cabinet at school, until the warning bell rang. I imagined we were there, in a familiar spot, as he kissed me again, playfully biting at my bottom lip.

We edged toward the bed, and just as I sat down, thighs spread, the sound of the creaking steps crept into the silence. We froze. As I stood, the sound quickened and grew louder. I surveyed the room. As I bent down to push an empty bottle under the bed, Mike moved swiftly, disappearing from my sight. My father pushed open the door. I sat on the ground by the bed, my tank top on, my bra off and on the other side of the room. My lips still tingled from the combination of Mike's soft mouth and hard liquor.

My father stood there in his work clothes and said nothing. I started rambling, saying I left school because I got in a fight with a girl. I felt something shift inside me as I spoke, as the woman I felt I was only moments before suddenly became a child again. I said I'd been scared. "She's a big girl, Dad. I thought she'd kill me if I stayed until the last bell."

Another good story, I thought, but I was hardly overconfident. I looked around the room, feeling a strange mix of worry and relief. It hit me that Mike might be seen when I noticed his shoes peeking out from behind the door; it was the only thing separating the two, they stood only a few feet apart, and if my father just glanced down, if he just pushed the door open another inch, there'd be an explosion and any harmony between us would fade into a memory.

My father stroked his beard, dark with the reddish hues of summer. "I want you to get yourself together and go back to school. I'll pick you up at the last bell. You can't run from a girl, no matter how big, or people like that will have you running the rest of your life."

He stared beyond me, to where my window was cracked and the sound of rain drops fell against the pane. My father wore the same dreamy expression a lot that year, since the paperwork for his divorce from my mother had been filed. Since then, in fact, I'd felt protective of him, as though our roles had been switched, and I reasoned that it would hurt him more than me if he found out. My older sister and father argued often, but between him and me, there was accord, and that couldn't change. I heard a rustling sound, Mike moving behind the door, and everything I felt toward him only seconds ago shifted toward momentary rage.

I watched my father closely for some reaction, but he merely continued to stare out the window. "Get yourself together," he said again as he closed the door and left.

As I got myself together, I whispered to Mike, explaining that my father never came home in the middle of his work day. He simply watched me, wide-eyed, and told me to go; he'd leave right after we did. I hoped he'd kiss me goodbye or cradle my chin in his hand and tell me he'd see me later, but instead, he just nodded at the door, nudged me out.

***

My father was already in the car, waiting, when I got downstairs. I walked to the door and noticed Mike's backpack sitting right next to mine, right next to the table where Dad always dropped his keys.

The ride to school was long, quiet, and the soft rock channel my father had chosen reminded me of the music that always played at the dentist's office. I wanted to tell him I was sorry, and that he had it all wrong, but how could I when he hadn't even addressed what he'd seen. Was it possible that he really didn't see Mike's backpack? That he really believed my story? When Dad dropped me off, he said nothing. As soon as I was out of the car, he took off as though he was in a drag race, and I hoped that Mike was long gone.

After the last bell, I searched for my father's green Honda, but somehow I knew it wouldn't be there. Although the incident would never come up, I could hear everything he might've said, a looping soundtrack in my mind, during the long bus ride home. I heard it again when my father and sister began arguing that night after she asked to stay out past curfew on Friday. When they began yelling, I retreated to my room and found the unopened bottles. I called Mike and asked him to meet him down the street before slipping out the back door, unnoticed. I thought.

Absurd Hunger

Vince was on his second gin and tonic when his phone began skidding across the bar, and although he was curious who was calling, he wasn't eager to answer. The skinny girl next to him, who had bought him this last round, picked it up. They'd barely gotten past their introductions and already she was handling his personal property. He thanked her and extended his hand, trying to remember whether or not she'd told him her name and then deciding, as she checked the number, it didn't matter.

"Vince? Hello, dear, it's Ela Dankowski." It took Vince a while to register the name, the shaky, familiar voice. "Now listen, I'm calling about your father."

Vince walked outside, hearing the girl behind him. "I knew he had a girlfriend."

"Mrs. Dankowski. It's been a long time."

This wasn't good. There was no reason for his father's neighbor to call unless there was some catastrophe. Vince braced himself for what he'd feel if she announced what he thought she might. He'd been meaning to call his father.

"Listen, Vince, you know I don't like to meddle, but your father needs someone to help him." She paused a moment, allowing Vince to digest the news. His guilt lifted as quickly as it came. The old man was still alive. "I don't know how else to say this, honey, but I think your father is losing his marbles. I don't mean to be so blunt, but—well, you just have to see him. He's a mess." She snorted.

Vince imagined his father's temper had got him in some sort of trouble. Throughout high school, Vince had been no stranger to accompanying his mother when she went to post bail for Wallace after another altercation. Once, his senior year, he'd even had the uncomfortable and embarrassing role of eyewitness in small claims court because his father had thrown a flowerpot at a minor. "What's he doing now?"

"He's just not himself. He's quiet." She could've stopped there. Wallace was a lot of things, but never quiet. "He won't talk, and his lawn is looking like hell. Vince, I know you've got a big life in Chicago. Your father told me all about your job and how hard you've been working, but I'm telling you, the man needs his son."

Aside from his legendary outbursts, Wallace had a reputation in the neighborhood for his gardening. He'd always, ever since Vince was a kid, spent his weekends planting flowers along the walkway, sectioning his garden for vegetables and herbs. Even in off-seasons, in the depth of Michigan's bitter winters, Wallace would spend hours at the kitchen table planning his landscape, sketching out his spring designs. He'd slowed down with age, sure, but even in recent years he toiled away at that yard, pruning and planting, guarding the area against small children and animals that threatened to destroy his art.

"Tell him I'm on my way."

"I'll tell him. I don't think he'll hear me though," she said.

If it weren't for a stroke of good timing, Vince might have talked himself out of the trip. Recently, he'd been fired from an upscale Italian restaurant. "You were one of the best in the kitchen, but I just can't afford to keep a cook who isn't accountable," Mr. Randazzo had said solemnly. Vince knew that his manager had been planning to fire him for some time. His suspicions were validated when he applied at a small bistro three blocks away, and the manager confided that Mr. Randazzo put the word out about Vince's performance. Figuring he'd been blacklisted from any decent paying job in the area, he simply stopped applying.

It isn't a tough decision to skip out on a lease there's no way of paying. But as Vince packed, he told himself he was doing what was right, for the right reasons.

***

Wallace was in a near-catatonic state when Vince arrived. Not only was he unresponsive, but he looked half-dead. There was a transparency to his skin and he'd lost weight, which made his face look long, his skin look too loose. Vince sat down at the kitchen table, across from Wallace, and apologized for not calling. When there was no response, he sifted through a short stack of unopened bills on the table, making awkward small talk, hoping that if he found the right topic, his father would come to life. All the things that his father had never shut up about: politics, food, gardening, the declining state of his neighborhood, went unanswered this day. Despite his own better judgment, Vince even put himself on the line, confessing, "You were right, Dad. I couldn't keep up in Chicago. They fired me." But Wallace didn't so much as look up, he kept his tired chin in his cupped hand and he continued to release shallow, sour breaths escaping between cracked, dry lips.

When Vince suggested a bath, Wallace followed him wordlessly, and submitted to his son's instructions like a child might, as though he'd forgotten how to execute this task on his own and he'd only been waiting for someone to offer. "Here, Dad, lift your arms. When's the last time you bathed?" Steel gray eyes fixed Vince in a terrifyingly vacant stare. Wallace's arms lifted, and Vince helped his father out of his clothes.

***

With the help of Mrs. Dankowski, Vince arranged a room for his father at a mental facility that took Medicare. He answered a psychologist's questions about his mother, her death a year ago, his father's relationship with her, and Wallace's general behavior patterns, including his documented anger issues and current medications—for blood pressure and cholesterol. The doctor, a tall, wiry man with small round glasses and an expressionless face, seemed most interested in Jacqueline. Vince explained that his mother had died in a messy highway car accident somewhere in Atlanta; that her body had been so mangled she'd been hard to identify, and the news had taken weeks to reach her family. She had been a passenger in the car her new boyfriend had been driving, and that he, too, had been killed. Reportedly, the accident was the fault of a teenager who was driving home drunk after a party. The teen had taken an illegal turn and collided head-on with his mother's car.

Although they had been separated when she died and they hadn't spoken but twice since the split, Wallace had made all the preparations for his wife's memorial. A few mutual friends attended, along with Jacqueline's parents, whom Wallace had been surprisingly tolerant of, if only for that one day.

"So he held himself together?" Dr. Randall asked.

"He held himself together then, did everything he was supposed to. He seemed to be coping well since, and even though she'd left him, he didn't seem to hold any grudges against her. He wouldn't allow me to say anything critical of her. It was a sore spot between us, and we would argue endlessly if I suggested that she wasn't coming back. He rationalized it by saying she was off 'finding herself'. He still thinks that it was only a matter of time before she returned and if her life hadn't been cut short, they would've reconciled."

Dr. Randall typed feverishly. When he was finished, he clasped his hands and leaned forward as though this were a clear cut case, there was an obvious diagnosis. He said that it sounded as though Wallace had never truly grieved the loss of his wife, not when she left him and definitely not when she died, and the momentum of his unaddressed feelings had ultimately pushed him into a corner and held him there. He seemed to be in the midst of a deep depression, and since he had no history of prior episodes like this, it was likely he'd be back to his old self with the proper treatment. He also told Vince that Wallace was severely malnourished and dehydrated when he arrived at the hospital. "If you hadn't have found him when you did, there's a good chance he'd be dead."

Wallace remained in the residence, monitored closely over the next two weeks. He was prescribed an antidepressant and, slowly, he began to talk again and, eventually, yell. Soon, Vince heard complaints that Wallace had been propositioning the nurses and arguing with the cafeteria staff about his food. When Vince was warned that his father would be asked to leave if he didn't stop acting out, Vince felt relief.

He continued to help Wallace out of his corner, a metaphor he often cited during this time, by adhering closely to the psychiatrist's recommendations. "Make sure he takes these pills before bed each night. Get him to my office at least two times a week. It'll take a while, but we'll get your father back," Dr. Randall said over the phone, after offering therapy on an individual basis only so that he didn't upset the staff or other residents.

"If he's propositioning nurses, he's already back," Vince told Dr. Randall.

Soon after his release, Wallace began to take walks and mind the front yard again. He returned to all his old routines, went to the IHOP each morning for eggs and bacon, barked orders at his son, complained about the teenagers who lived down the street, invited young women to "Give it a go with an experienced man." Vince credited the medication for such a dramatic improvement in a matter of weeks, but he also felt, on some level, that his father still needed him around. Despite the return of the old man's sharp tongue, there were some mornings when Wallace backed up, temporarily, into that corner again, when his gaze went inward and something in him disappeared, something that hadn't been there the day Vince returned.

When word got around that Vince was back from Chicago, he was offered his old part-time job at Mercer's, which he immediately accepted. The restaurant, a family-style diner that his parents used to run, offered little money, but it was enough to save. And it was remarkable how quickly he fell into his old routines.

***

09/06

Dear Jacqueline,

This is stupid. You're dead and I'm supposed to write you a letter. Some new-agey hack named Dr. Randall insisted I do this.

He says I haven't grieved properly, that I have unresolved feelings toward you (no shit!) and that this might help. You should see the guy. He's skinny with a big nose, broken blood vessels all over it like he's an old boozer or something, not to mention the fact that he's old! Almost as old as me. He suggested I start doing yoga, too. Can you imagine? You're probably thinking—or not thinking at all since you're dead and this is ridiculous—that I'm a fool, but I don't really have a choice. My freedom's on the line, kid. I was in a fucking mental institution for weeks. Felt like years.

Truth is, I really did get a little crazy there. You were a woman, so you know what that's like. I got stuck on this thought, felt like I had a riddle to solve. It wasn't painful or anything, but I stopped noticing time. I would wake up and then the thought would come. I had to save someone and I couldn't figure out who or how, and I'd sit down somewhere to think about it and next thing I'd know, I'd be waking up again.

By the way, your son's living with me again. He's probably out of money or wouldn't have come back. I'm letting him think that he saved his old man's life. Truth is, when he came home, I was starting to feel better anyway. I was about to snap out of it. I'll let him be a hero in his own mind. I suppose he needs something to be proud of. I miss you, kid. I miss your gumbo. Maybe I just miss the gumbo. Fuck this shit.

Wallace

***

09/21

Dear Jacqueline,

I'm writing you again. Dumb shit. Psychobabble. Bullshit. Probably.

I'm getting fat again, girl. I think it's these meds they have me on. I feel like I'm dragging around weights, and I'm eating everything in sight. I go to IHOP and even that doesn't fill me up. I'm tired all the time.

You know it's all your fault, right? Remember how you used to force those salads and vegetables on me? And back then I wasn't even that big. Well, no one does that now and so I'm fucked. I'm fucked in a lot of ways with you not around. I miss you, girl.

I don't know why you decided to die so fast, leave me with your fuckhead son to take care of. I know you always said he was just a late bloomer, but he's in his thirties now, and I'm not seeing it. He can't keep a job.

What made you leave, Jacki? Was it another man? The man in the car? Don't answer. I know you were coming back. So why'd you die? Your dying makes no sense. Without you, life is just a bunch of days going by, a bunch of things to do. I guess it goes to show how bad things are that I'm even writing you these letters. I'm writing to my dead wife. I feel worse now. Hear that, Dr. Randall? I feel worse than I did before you told me to do this. Thanks for that. I hope you ask to read it. Or you better yet, when I die, I'll leave it to you in my will.

I'll keep this notebook on me. I want you to know, for future reference, just how pointless this is, it's cruel.

Wallace

***

10/05

Dear Jacqueline,

You remember when I used to take our kid to the rec center to play basketball? I used to watch him and worry the bigger kids would beat him up, but I couldn't do anything if they did (they'd know better than to do it in front of me. I'd kick any kid's ass if he touched my son). Then I found him sneaking my Maker's Mark at sixteen and I worried he'd take to the sauce like your father. I worried he wouldn't use a condom, get some girl pregnant, and then when he didn't, I thought he was gay. I wouldn't mind a gay son; tell you the truth, because at least he'd have a primary income in his household, someone to take care of him.

You remember how I'd have nightmares then, vivid, realistic, about his sensitive, worrisome ass coming home at thirty, strung out like all these crack heads around here. I mean, why wouldn't he? He was easily swayed. He couldn't keep a job. Well, for the first time in my life, I don't feel like that about him. Something's changing in the boy. He's a late bloomer, sure, but I think he's finally growing up.

By the way, I had a good talk with Maggie yesterday, you remember her? The girl at IHOP. She might've been assistant manager back when you were around. We talked about how meaningless all this shit is—life—and how we make our own reality. So, fuck Dr. Randall's reasoning. I'll write for my own damn reasons. I still love you and this is all I have.

I still wake up thinking about you, girl. Your side of the bed feels warm some days, like you were there with me. It's tough to explain, but I think that maybe if I keep believing that side of the bed is yours, I'll convince myself that it is. For a few seconds time stops again, and I forget you're gone. Sometimes I think I'm losing it again. But time hasn't left me completely.

Ha! I'm sappy as hell. If only I could've come up with some of this shit before you left. Maybe you'd have stayed. Too little, too late. Maybe Vince gets that late bloomer thing from me.

I love you, girl.

(Dr. Randall, go fuck yourself. I'm doing this for my own reasons. I'm down to a forth of a pill a day. I've been flushing the rest, just so I don't have to hear it from Vince. Dr. Randall, if you read this, go fuck yourself. Twice.)

Wallace

***

11/1

Dearest,

The neighborhood is going to hell in a hand basket. Ela Dankowski's house was broken into last night. Not only did they rob her, they beat her up! An old woman. Jacqueline, girl, I'm not putting up with this anymore. I can't afford to. Your son (he's definitely your son!) mentioned how much better I seemed, how he might start looking for a new job again.

He's talking about leaving for North Carolina. Some hot shit restaurant there. Somehow he thinks he can get the chef gig right off the bat. He's not that good a cook, is he? Maybe so. You'd come back to me if you had the chance, I know. I know he will, too, but I can't afford for him to leave. Just like that. Something has to change.

(Fuck you, Dr. Randall, our last session was a fucking joke—no shit my dreams mean I'm going through a transition. People are always going through transitions. I wrote up a will on my son's computer today and you're getting these letters. By the way, I'm off the pills. Fucking electric zaps you warned me about, yeah, feeling those, but I also lost ten pounds. I get dizzy, suppose because you've made me into a legal crack head and I'm in withdrawal. Why the fuck do you all think medicine is the answer, can't you look back and see how wrong that was? Heroine, coke, all that shit was prescribed by assholes like you. Fuckhead!)

Love,

Wallace

***

Vince was exhausted. He'd been working double shifts at the restaurant, and he wasn't sure how much of this conversation he was dreaming. He wished he was dreaming. Wallace was sitting in the bedroom, his large, shadowy body rocking slightly as he rambled on nonsensically, about some plan to get Jacqueline back. Vince told his father to go to sleep, he pleaded, but Wallace responded, "I'll fight for her, boy. I will." After repeating this a few more times, there was a long silence.

Vince awoke again when his father yelled, "They won't stop me from doing this. They won't lock me up."

"Dad, we'll talk about it in the morning," Vince said. As much as his father's insanity saddened him, he couldn't help but to think that it was he, Vince, who was screwed. Thanks to the old man, he was destined to stay here forever. And, as he began to fall out of consciousness again, Vince thought about how appreciated he was at work. Mercer's was a small diner, and it didn't pay much; consequently, the place didn't attract cooks who took pride in their work. The customers had been praising him, the servers had been thanking him for bigger tips, and there was even a cute little girl there… but Vince couldn't think about that now. Not now.

Wallace watched his son fall asleep, but he didn't stop talking. He included every detail, illustrated each point of action with small, uneven circles and squares, initials for street names and arrows pointing in every direction. He mentioned potential dates and times, explaining that weather conditions might alter the agenda slightly. He went on like this until the stagnant, dusty air in his own house turned his voice into a scratch. By this time, Vince was snoring. He probably wouldn't remember a word and, Wallace reasoned, maybe this was best.

***

10/13

Dear Jacqueline,

Things are moving quickly now. The days. I've made plans to see you.

I ran down my plan, just in case, and I wouldn't have done that if I didn't trust the boy now. I think he's growing up. He's kept his job for sometime. I'm on the ball again, kid, like I used to be. I'm going to put on a show for you. You better be watching because I'm sure it'll go down any day now.

By the way, I know you never liked being compared to other women, so when I told IHOP Maggie that she reminded me of you — if you saw that — please don't take it the wrong way. Everything reminds me of you lately. I feel like we're closer to each other than ever before.

See you soon, kid.
Love,
Wallace

***

Wallace fumbled with his key a while before getting the lock to turn. He wasn't surprised to find Jacqueline on the couch. She was reading one of the silly romance novels sold in the impulse aisles of the grocery store. She thumbed through the book with her eyes glazed over in a way he imagined they'd be if she ever watched porn with him the way he wanted her to. "I've been thinking about you all day," he said.

"Good. Hey, just let me finish this chapter, and then we'll talk, okay?"

"Listen, woman, I need to talk now. I want to tell you about this dream I had last night. It was the past and I'm not with you yet. Only felt like the future, not the past. When I woke up, I felt like I was moving backwards."

"Wallace, darling, you make no sense. You start analyzing your dreams like that and the next thing you know you'll be asking me to go get our palms read together. Have you seen Dr. Randall this week?"

"I'm losing it. Fine." She looked up at him with a half-smile and he read her thought. "Or already lost it. Whatever. Listen, I need to know… If I'm really losing it for good, you'll hire me a hot nurse, right?"

"Jesus, Wallace! Give me five minutes. This is my meditative time, me time, you hear? Just five minutes then you'll have my undivided attention."

Wallace eyed his wife's pale legs, the thick purple veins that slid up from her ankles like snakes.

"Have it your way, beautiful," he said, heading toward the kitchen, where he found a pot of gumbo simmering, thickening the air around him.

"Oh shut up, Wallace," she yelled after him, but he could hear the lightness to her voice, the hint of appreciation.

As she read, Wallace did his rounds. He checked the drawers, the closet, the fridge, and all his ammunition was in place. He owned a shotgun and two 9mms that he rotated weekly, just in case someone was scoping the house. He kept two bullets in an egg carton in the fridge and a gun taped to the wall behind it—this one rarely moved as there were fewer places to hide a gun in a kitchen than in other rooms. As he made his rounds, he began to think about his dream again and whether the insight he'd had on the bus was connected to the dream. Therapy was turning him into a nut, and he knew he had to protect his wife now. That people were trying to take her away. He checked the ottoman for a Swiss Army knife that was kept underneath a few old newspapers. He tapped on Jacqueline's thick legs, which lifted so that he could check under the couch for a few hand weights, strategically placed. He was proud to say he could still lift the ten pounders and throw them easy enough.

Quite satisfied, he took a seat next to Jacqueline and closed his eyes. Time seemed still again. When his son returned, he was too tired to engage the boy. He was beginning to feel less guilty about checking out from time to time.

***

Wallace sat in a leather chair that reclined. It was the kind of chair he'd been hoping to one day purchase just for football Sundays and the occasional episode of Judge Judy. He'd been cutting back on daytime TV lately. In a way, this chair was his now. It was always waiting for him, each morning. Often, he'd show up early just to enjoy the comfort a bit longer. He'd read from the daily paper there with a cup of decaffeinated coffee—the only kind served in the place—and settle in, sometimes for an hour, until the doctor arrived. It wasn't just the chair that Wallace enjoyed, but the entire room. Classical music or musak, as he'd heard it referred, was always barely audible in the backdrop and the room itself was as harmonious as the smooth, quiet rhythms. There was a couch that matched the leather chair he favored, and a decorative fireplace. Two oil paintings hung on the walls, large and full of yellows and dark blues that didn't depict a sunset but gave Wallace the distinct feeling that he was watching one. He didn't notice his son come in.

The room, Wallace thought, would be exactly what he'd have had he been a wealthy man. It would be his den, or even his front room, and he would discourage guests from sitting in it. It would be his room, his sanctuary, where he would have what Jacqueline used to refer to as me time.

The room Wallace slept in now wasn't nearly as nice as this, but it, too, had a serene feel. The facility that Vince arranged for him was a rehabilitated monastery. There were high ceilings with narrow windows built in, and breathtaking stained glass windows. The very air in the place was thick with comfort; even the food was good.

"I knew I'd find you here," Vince said. "You have an hour before your appointment. You want to get some breakfast at IHOP?"

Wallace felt his stomach shift at the very mention of IHOP. He knew his son's intentions were good, but the last thing he wanted to do was leave. "Why not just sit with my crazy ass and have some decaf? It's not half bad if you put some cinnamon and sugar in it. Here," he pulled out a baggie filled with brown capsules. "Here, real cinnamon. Jacqueline tells me that stuff you buy at the store is not cinnamon; it's not as good, not as fine texturally. I used to buy these capsules or go to the spice store and buy a bottle of the good stuff when I made cinnamon pear tortes. Did I ever make those for you?"

"I brought you that cinnamon, Dad, not Jacqueline, not Mom."

Wallace nods. "Did I? Did I ever make those tortes for you?"

"No."

"It's been a long time. Your mother loves them."

Loved them, Dad, Vince thought. "I know, Dad." Vince watched his father's gaze as it fell somewhere beyond his grasp and he seemed settled there. Vince was working a lot, taking care of his father, paying bills, managing things. Life wasn't great, but he was doing what he was supposed to. He knew his father was proud to rely on his son, even if he wasn't sure how to express it. "I saw what you did with the garden. The lady at the front desk, Anita, I think, she was so excited about what you did. She told me how flirtatious you were with her, how she didn't mind much because you'd brought their little garden back to life. She didn't understand your insistence on sunflowers, but she said that she was ordering in anything you wanted. She called you a genius."

"That chunky little girl wants a piece of me," Wallace said. "Don't tell your mother."

"I'm sure. Anyway, the garden looks good. You sure you don't want to go get a bite to eat, get out of here for a few minutes?"

"You see this," Wallace said, pointing around the room. "This is my living room. This is my home."

Vince put his arm around Wallace and rested his hand on his father's shoulder.

Wallace knew the boy thought he was crazy. He could tell by the way they spoke now, as though Wallace was the child and Vince was the father. Something about the way everyone spoke to Wallace now, even Jacqueline, the way everyone was so gentle and accommodating, was oddly nice, addictive even. In a way, he wanted to egg it on, to make sure it would last. This new home, the care, even the bullshit therapy sessions in which he was made to talk about his dreadful past, how it was different than the present, it was all so unthreatening, so inconsistent with reality.

He wanted to thank his son, but there was too much to thank him for; his gift had been too complex, too all-encompassing to acknowledge with mere words. The two sat in their chairs and drank decaf coffee remaining, for the most part, quiet. And when Wallace would glance over at his son, he saw, finally, the boy's ability to appreciate the silence as much as he did, and he knew that the boy was learning, finally beginning to understand how important it is to be still.

The Millers

Desiree never said much, at least not to the Millers, even though they had been watching her after school for months. She didn't think she had much to say. Biting her bottom lip, always, sometimes hard enough to pierce a small, circular wound into it, she listened to them. She listened to each gossipy word that dripped from Mrs. Miller's nonstop mouth. She received an unsolicited education on the indiscretions and strange obsessions of many adults who lived on the street, many of whom she had seen often, but hoped now she would never meet. Always a polite girl, Desiree nodded when the woman paused to take a breath and smiled on cue.

When Desiree's mother returned from work, the sun would be giving way to the crisp air of night, and the girl would feel a flutter of nervous energy in her stomach. As soon as the phone would ring, she'd grab her small plastic backpack and run home where she would begin to talk incessantly, repeating the more interesting tidbits that Mrs. Miller has shared with her.

Desiree felt like a vessel, whose sole purpose was to transport words from Mrs. Miller's mouth to her mother's ears, if only for entertainment value. When her mother inquired about what Desiree had done that day, she only ventured original conversation about what happened after school. She talked of the obscene red color Mrs. Miller had dyed her hair, or the gut-twisting cookies she served so proudly. "They're sugar free," Desiree would repeat in Mrs. Miller's nasally voice. This would make her mother laugh. Desiree told her mother about the musty smell of Mr. Miller's garage; the way he never looked at his wife as she rambled on and how instead, he directed his gaze to Desiree and asked her how things were at home. These mundane details seemed to hold her mother's interest more than anything else. So she would repeat the few words Mr. Miller had said, "Hi, there, young lady. Tough day at work?" or "One thing about watching you neighbor kids, you always seem to make an old man feel young again."

"He's a kind man," her mother said.

"Yeah, he never makes me eat carrot-flavored cookies. He never puts me to work the way Mrs. Miller does." Desiree watched the way her mother fumbled to light her long, skinny cigarettes, and how she nodded at the appropriate pauses in speech, just as Desiree had when she was listening to Mrs. Miller. She told her mother that Mr. Miller had been fixing up a bike for one of their neighbors, and that it growled like a tiger now when a week ago it wouldn't even start. Her mother's eyes, the color of wet clay, seemed to lighten a shade at the mention of Mr. Miller. She went on, "You know, Mom, he always asks about you. He asks if you seem happy." To this, a smile spreads across her mother's face.

This is when the idea was born. Desiree, bored throughout much of school would begin to write. She would tell Mr. Miller how her mother seemed happy when she spoke of him. She would tell him small details about her mother, like what she wore or how tired she had been from waitressing that day. Maybe she'd tell him that her mother had inquired about him, too. What could it hurt?

The Probability of Him

Sarah's yellow summer dress blew against her long, tanned legs as she sifted through a flower pot half-filled with gravel. I wondered how she could be so comfortable as to bend over in something so short. I had a similar dress, a blue one, and the one day I wore it to school, I'd been so worried about the thing blowing up or getting stuck in the back of my panties, that I ended up walking home for lunch just to change.

I massaged my temples as my sister brushed off a half-smoked cigarette and followed my gaze, which had settled on the boy across the street. She laughed.

"Make your move," she said.

"Yeah right."

"You'll never learn to be a lady if you don't practice now, during the, urm, developing stages of your sexuality." She looked down at my mud-laced tennis shoes and baggy jeans as I pushed the swing back and held it there.

"I'm not thinking about that boy. I'm thinking about my algebra homework."

"He's more important," she said. I watched as Sarah lit the butt, took a long drag and sat on the porch step watching the boy. It seemed as though she were trying to will him to look her way. He flipped his skateboard up under his arm and inspected its underside. He tried to spin one of the wheels and it barely moved. The boy was new to the neighborhood and there was something about him that I liked, maybe the fact that he hadn't hit on my sister. His body was angular and thin; his face freckled and pale. My sister whispered that she found nothing attractive about him, but it interested her that he hadn't even bothered to look our way.

"You're staring," I said. "It's probably freaking him out."

"He's fascinating. Okay, Algebra 101: If X is hot and Y is ignoring her, then Y is what? Gay?"

"I'm getting a D in algebra," I said.

"Mmmmm. Maybe not gay. Maybe he's slow. Maybe his eyesight is poor, no peripheral vision…"

I figured quite the opposite. People didn't not notice my sister. The boy had probably picked up on the fact that the pretty, fast-ass looking girl across the street was watching him, and to lure her in, he was playing hard to get. "Not every boy is interested in you," I lied.

"We'll see," Sarah said. She licked her bottom lip and bit it.

"Go ask him out then," I said, hoping she wouldn't.

"You think I won't?"

"I don't think he's interested."

"Excuse me," Sarah called out to the boy, who turned around and his thin, wide mouth curled up in a half-smile. It was his mouth that I concentrated on. He nodded hello, and much to my dismay, sized her up as she crossed the street.

Sarah said something and pointed toward me, or our house. His eyes did not follow her directive.

For a moment, I felt like I was watching the Nature Channel. My sister might as well have been mewing and lifting her tail. But the boy seemed less interested after a short exchange, and ultimately, he broke their mutual gaze to look up at me. The bottom of my feet began to tingle as he smiled; the moment hung heavily until long after the boy turned around. My sister returned to the porch, shaking her head.

"Shot down?"

Sarah hit me with her bony fist, causing my forearm to sting. "What, you think it's funny?" I realized the smile I had returned to the boy hadn't left my face. "That boy probably suffered some trauma; he probably saw something horrible and suffers from post-traumatic stress, which causes him to retreat into himself," my sister said. "He can't relax, and doesn't allow himself the pleasures of youth."

My mother is a psychologist and she used to make a game of labeling people we all knew, telling us her theories upon first glance. It was highly unprofessional, I thought, but the game was addictive. It made every person a mystery, a riddle that could be solved with history, behavior and body language. Usually, our diagnoses lacked factual reasoning—the history portion—but this only made it more fun. "Maybe he just doesn't find narcissistic teenage girls attractive," I said.

It turns out that it wasn't the past that haunted the boy, but the present. He had Leukemia. He was hospitalized for the last time soon after the day my sister approached him. When Sarah heard the news, she nodded. "I knew it had to be something… I mean, he just cut me off that day and asked if I'd leave him alone. Chronic disease explains everything."

"You couldn't be more full of yourself."

She shrugged. "Did you pass your test?"

"72%."

"See, my algebra lesson paid off that day."

I hit my sister on her shoulder. The blow surprised us both, and for a brief second I didn't think she'd retaliate. Before I knew it, though, I was ground-level, with size six boots pummeling my sides.

I was still sore when I attended the boy's funeral. If you would've asked me why I went, I couldn't have said. I stood among a small group of people I didn't know, wearing sunglasses to hide a yellowing bruise, listening to heartfelt tributes to a boy I never spoke to. Everyone around me was crying—or looking like they wanted to—and offering each other comforting half-smiles. I found out that the boy's name was Danny. He was sixteen, the same age as Sarah. He was a photographer and skater, a bit of a daredevil. I thought about the way he'd looked at me, with a photographer's eye, as though I were a mystery he wanted to solve. And I felt my eyes begin to swell as I joined in mourning this boy I never got to know, who never got to know me, because we missed our chance.

Cheers

Robert was offered a position in Texas. A day later, I found myself stuffing my wardrobe into a few bags, giving away furniture—one television, two lamps, a bamboo rug, and an underutilized hall tree—and asking for a work transfer. I called everyone I knew with the big news, but my reportage was met with a bombardment of assumption.

"So when is the wedding?"

The question caught me off-guard the first time I was asked, but soon the repetition and awkwardness of it evoked irritation, something like the metal scrape of a dentist's pick as it moves along the gum line.

I realize that it is a fair question, a somewhat fair assumption. When two people are in a long-term relationship, the discussion of marriage seems inevitable. But Robert and I agreed that we didn't want to ruin our relationship with a set of shiny rings and stamped approval from the state. We didn't believe in changing things for no reason, and definitely not to fit into some social or societal norm or to appease friends. Okay, so this last part was my internal dialogue, but Robert agreed that he, too, was happy with the way things were. We began responding to such probing inquiries with locked eyes, a conspiratorial smile, and the statement that we were happy as "partners."

***

We set out for the Lone Star State as partners. We drove on different days, taking a parallel path, stopping only once before reaching our destination, a place where we would meet again, where we knew no one else, San Antonio, Texas. It was a lively city, the seventh largest, at the time, with a transient population of military transients and tourists, those emigrating from Mexico and many moving north from El Paso, and a few natives. The temperature always seemed just a few degrees warmer than perfect, while the traffic was always jelly-tight on the windy roads that all seemed to lead to endless shopping and food.

Our new apartment was near downtown, small, cheap, and conveniently close to an outrageous number of diverse and fabulous restaurants and bars. Everything was just down the street, it seemed. Everyone seemed polite. The new energy of a new city was enlivening, stimulating. We were scared out of our minds.

***

I was eleven. It was 1990 and my mother was alone, sneaking a cigarette at the kitchen window before my father got home. I walked in. She exhaled out the window, the same way I would when I turned fourteen and began sneaking her cigarettes up to my room. Mom had combined the last of our ketchup, some bread crumbs, half an onion, a huge chunk of ground beef and a few eggs in a big bowl. She threw the oven mitt at me. "You can finish the meatloaf," she said as she lit another cigarette. I wondered how the need to smoke had interrupted her at such an awkward point in the food preparation. I looked at the pinkish-brown meat laced with yolk and refused my mother's request, scrunching my face for emphasis before running out of the room. I hated helping her cook.

When my father arrived home, the meatloaf was in the oven, filling the house with the smell of onions and comfort. He said hello and walked upstairs to change. I helped Mom set the table.

She sat, picking at her own plate as she watched my father eat his meal. He patted his stomach and burped.

"You're welcome," Mom said. She meant it. I laughed. Meanwhile, Mom continued to watch my father closely as he ate. He never returned her gaze. He wouldn't speak to her again during the meal.

***

I used to stare at the wall of our living room, which was adorned with African masks and my father's art. When they were still dating, Dad drew Mom's body in sections, charcoal outlines of her thigh or the side of her arm, her waist, framed grayscale pictures. Those portraits were a series of framed mysteries. I didn't understand their symbolism, and I remember searching for familiar lines in the shading. I wanted to figure them out, but only my parents knew which picture was the outline of an arm, the side of hip. I could only make out shapes. These pictures were without story. Only my parents could see the story alone, and yet neither Mom nor Dad stared at them the way I did.

***

Robert and I began to realize that knowing no one, in a new city, was tough. We argued over the idea of moving back, finding another job. Although we loved San Antonio, the feeling of being on a busy island was sinking us. We suffered from a mild case of culture shock—what are all these people smiling about?--along with the environmental confusion when there was no snow in the winter and very little rain in the spring. We longed for friends and family, and green plants. Slowly, however, we assimilated.

We made a home out of our one-bedroom apartment and adopted a dog, a blue heeler, which we spoiled with table scraps and a place at the foot of our bed. We laughed and waved to each other on the nights we would awaken to awkward positions, the dog wedged between us, snug under the covers, taking up most of the bed. We began touring the city, finding adventure in the endless windy roads that all seemed to end at another great place to eat, another glass of wine, another talk about the future. Eventually, we made a few friends, none of which knew us well enough yet to hassle us about our marital status.

***

I was thrilled to see my father again, six months after the move. He remarried since divorcing my mother almost fifteen years ago, but lately—only lately—he began telling me stories about his love affair with Mom. This day, he told me about the time the two took an entire summer to make things from scratch. They made cheese, bread, and three kinds of wine in their small apartment in Toledo, Ohio.

"That raisin wine was a chore," he said, laughing. A dark piece of straight, limp hair fell low on his forehead and he pushed it back. He needed a haircut. We sat opposite each other in a booth at Denny's, neither of us happy with our meal.

"We drove all the way around the city, just looking for raisins. I think there was a grape shortage—the one summer I can remember in history that there has been a grape shortage! And we picked that summer to make our wine."

Dad went on to say that they needed a lot of raisins for the recipe and that they drove for hours looking for them. He recalled laughing the first few times they stopped at stores with no raisins, or not enough raisins. For some reason, their goal was to fill a large plastic tub so as not to alter the recipe they had acquired—one that made a few gallons. As they slowly amassed the stock at various markets and grocers around the city, they only got more determined. They listened to loud music and laughed, kissed, sang. They drove that day with growing desire. Mom's chestnut-colored hair was long then, and I imagine it blowing around as they drove. I imagine my father, his beard full-grown and his hair even longer than it is now.

"Man, that wine was nasty," he said. "But we did it. It was a lot of fun." Dad laughed, looking toward reminiscence; that spot another's eyes can't quite trace.

Perhaps such memories snubbed those of discontentment that they shared during the dinners I remember as a child—disconnection, longing. I pictured Mom's deeply-tanned face at that dinner table, longing for her husband's recognition. I saw my father's inability to appease her, to make her feel loved; I saw her refusal to please him, to lose weight and stop spending money, to quit smoking.

***

It wasn't long before my father found love. It seemed easy for him, as though love was there waiting for him to return to it. And maybe it was; maybe love is always waiting. Or maybe it's always waiting for men.

I have seen this phenomenon often in my family; the patriarch—widowed or divorced—remarried within a year of the divorce. It is as though the Maxwell men got a taste for marriage and stuck with the idea, rather than the women. Mom, on the other hand, decided against a second marriage. She attached a different meaning to the word, one that was more extreme, less interpretive, perhaps less romantic.

***

I was still wary of the concept of marriage, and at the same time eager to approach my relationship in a clear, straightforward way; what is marriage, after all, if not a business agreement to be faithful to one another? It is an agreement made at love's apex, so the contract is bound by the assumption that love's momentum will continue to renew itself, peaking again and again, or else stabilize while remaining appealing to both partners. Marriage is a promise to control future events and this promise is not always realistic. Love is a promise we can't always keep.

Perhaps it's the trauma associated with the loss of love that my mother has to recover from, not the marriage itself, but she still seems hurt when we talk about her marriage to my father. She will find love again, a psychic recently told her, but she laughed it off. For now, she has resolved not to remarry. She says she feels less alone than she did when she was married.

"Do you remember making raisin wine with Dad?" I asked her.

Her face, still tan, somewhat broader, somehow brighter, lit up more. "That was a great summer," she said. "You're father and I drove around all day. We were on a mission and we weren't going to give up for anything." She, too, said something about the disgusting taste of the wine, but remembered drinking it fondly.

***

I told Robert about the wine and suggested we try it. We purchased 1 lb of sugar, 2lbs of raisins, and a lemon.

"Maybe we shouldn't do this," I said. "You know, it didn't work out so well for them."

"It's easy," he responded, reaching for the instructions by my computer screen. "We add 6 quarts of boiling water to these ingredients then we just have to stir it every day. In a month, we'll have wine." Robert kissed me on the cheek, and reminded me that they probably just did it wrong.

We stood in the kitchen, hovering over a large glass bowl. I instructed Robert to stir as I poured. I noticed that his beard was growing back in, shading his jaw, his olive-hued skin, with subtle shadows. I've always found this stage of a beard attractive on him, masculine, natural and fleeting. He had to keep a clean-shave for his job now, so this look was a rarity, reserved for long weekends and holidays.

"I can't guarantee this will be good," I said, handing him a wooden spoon.

Robert bent his knees until his eyes were in-line with my own. He rested his arm on my shoulder and I felt the length of the spoon down my back. "It's worth a shot," he said.

I agreed.

Negligence

Jerrod traced his thumb along the smooth chin line of his perfect little girl. Not only the bluest eyes, the loudest laugh, the smallest arms, she was also a juggler, a Rubik's cube master, a mere nine years old with no makeup lines. Jerrod was no longer self-conscious about being the only man who signed his daughter up for Texas beauty pageants; he knew this distinction granted him special treatment, a seat at the front of the stage, a new scholarship for his girl.

Little Greta was a namesake, the third generation, but not a "third" or "junior." Jerrod couldn't fathom putting her in line behind her predecessors. The glimmer in her was the very same glimmer that had existed in her mother, who had died during childbirth. Jerrod fixed a mahogany curl in his daughter's left pigtail and stood back, taking her in, her miniature perfection.

A mother with wide eyes and soft-looking, porcelain skin approached. "What a beauty," she said, appreciating Greta with feigned awe, which Jerrod believed to be genuine.

"Is your daughter competing?"

"Yes, Michaelina was first runner-up last year. We doubt she can compete with Greta, but her hair has grown quite long, so pretty and thick. We think she's grown out of her awkward stage."

Jerrod looked over at a red-haired girl with eyes like her mother's, only greener, larger in proportion to her face. He found the girl's perfect little dimples immediately threatening. For some reason he couldn't fathom, freckles were in style now. "Great skin," he said.

"Aloe. We put it in everything. It's a family secret, but I don't mind telling you."

"What's her talent?" Jerrod asked.

"Gymnastics. Check her out; she'll be up first today. She can do some pretty impressive back flips. We practice at the pool."

"A pool?" Greta chimed, "Can we go?"

The woman laughed. "Sure, princess. My name is Sophia. You can come over and swim with me anytime. You can even bring your father along, if you'd like." She slipped a business card out of her purse and into Jerrod's hand. "Anytime."

"It has been a while since we've been swimming," he said. He noticed her full bottom lip briefly as she bit down on it in an endearing, nervous fashion. His mind had not ventured in the manner she evoked in some time. He wanted to embrace her, her nervous, soft body, and gently kiss that lip, bite it himself.

As the woman walked off, switching her weight with deliberate exaggeration, Jerrod refocused, and yelled out to Greta, "Come on, sweetie, let's go check out the stage."

Jerrod examined the area, finding Greta the best place to stand. "There, right there. Your face will be in the judges' optical center, like a perfect photograph," he said. Jerrod opened a bottle of lotion and smacked it against his palm. A large amount fell onto the stage, far to the right of the optical center. He wiped it, spreading it around with a napkin. The pinkish, greasy liquid became less noticeable, but left a wide, slippery spot. He considered the spot a moment, told himself it would not realistically hurt anyone. It might even dry up. He could get something more to wipe it up, or alert someone behind the scenes, but instead he chose to leave it; a simple act of negligence for which he would never forgive himself.

Levity

I recounted missed appointments, work shifts and cat feedings along with a series of forgotten door codes, keys, vitamins, and days in which I had forgotten to apply deodorant or moisturizer. Dr. Randall listened patiently, fiddling with his round glasses as I went down my list. When I finished, he said, "Maybe you're depressed." He asked me if I had any traumatic experiences in my past. I said no. He offered me anti-depressants. I said no. He recommended other avenues to pursue, and gave me the number of a neurologist, in case things got worse.

"Whatever it is in your head, blocking your recall," a hypnotherapist told me, "it must be addressed in order for you to be cured." The underlying meaning of this, I thought, was that if I did not respond to her services it would be my fault. I tried. I sat on a light blue couch and tried to imagine my eyelids were heavy and the cushions beneath me were clouds. She said, "Ten. You are sinking into relaxation... feel your muscles relaxing. Nine. Your thoughts are slowing, your breath is slow. Eight. Feel your body sink..." And all I could think about was my car, a standard, and whether or not I'd remembered to pull the emergency break—this was one of the many examples I can give you of my minor glitches of memory; minor glitches that could lead to major upset. I ran out of the room and across the street to my car, forgetting to look both ways and almost got creamed by a white SUV. I found my car still parked, but the emergency break had not been lifted.

The neurologist that Dr. Randall recommended ran a series of tests that showed no signs of Alzheimer's or brain tumors, but some couldn't be done because the insurance money ran out. In fact, it didn't take long before my entire savings was depleted due to this diagnostic quest. I ended up having to return my car to the dealership, which also turned out badly because it meant I now had bus schedules to memorize. What I was prescribed were "tools" to help me cope with memory loss, like mnemonic games to play and crossword puzzles. I was diligent: I kept lists of things to do on the fridge, and worked my crossword puzzles during my lunch break at the bank. I don't mean a financial institution. I worked at a blood bank or, more specifically, a plasma donation center.

I never forgot how to do my job, how to tie a piece of tan rubber at the base of a bicep and instruct the donor to pump his fist until the vein rises like a small blue wave. I had the best record at the bank for clean sticks. I only missed a vein once, which, for my years of service, was rather outstanding, if I do say so myself. For this reason alone, my boss forgave the few times I came in on my day off or for the wrong shift because I remembered the bus or work schedule wrong. A missed shift here and there, he told me, was better than a blown vein, which causes the donor excessive bruising and a generally pissy mood. At the same time, he warned, if this continued I'd lose my job.

***

His card came to me serendipitously. I was smoking a cigarette, and as I dropped it and went to grind it out with my heel, I saw a white and gold business card, wind-pushed beneath the lit butt.

"Fire," a customer said, offering me her arm after I told her I was a Leo, an August baby. "You are fiery, I can tell. Fire signs are the signs of life and action, but also the signs of danger." The woman's veins were generous and the needle slid in easily as she continued, "I'm Desiree, a Pisces; we're prone to laziness—if only I had the opportunity!" She laughed at herself and explained that she was no hack. Desiree had been studying astrology for two years, and she assured me it was a science that would make my head spin, if I only knew its complexity.

I nodded. "I might get a reading one day, but can't right now. Maybe you'll be doing readings yourself by the time I can afford it?"

"I would love to read you," she said. "But yeah, it'll be a while."

I smiled. "Enjoy the movie," I said, offering her headphones and directing her gaze to the small flat screen TV perched above a row of chairs at the end of the room. I saw Will Smith's face flash across the screen, then a shot of people running. I took my seat at the end of the row. Waiting, watching people watch half an action movie as their blood pumped into an IV bag, drained of plasma and pumped right back in, was the part of the job I truly despised. We always had the same action movies playing, and no one ever looked interested. They all looked impatient and calculating, as though they were already mentally spending the eighty or thirty-five dollar check we'd cut them after the Band-Aid.

I pulled the business card from the back pocket of my jeans. My cigarette butt had scorched its edge. The card read only, "Healer," above an address not far from my apartment complex. I watched the astrologer, a small, intense woman with frizzy dark hair, roll her eyes at something on the TV screen, and I tried desperately to remember whether or not she'd told me her name.

I felt a lightness the rest of the work day, and as I sat at my post between clean sticks, I continuously fingered the card as though it were some sort of talisman. It was the four leaf clover I kept in my grade school notebook until I accidentally left it on the bus; the silver medallion my mother had given me when she was sick, a symbol of good luck, she'd said, I'd believed—before she had her last stroke. Now, I had a business card, a possibility, and I worried that if I went to the address printed on its front my fantasy would be weighed down by reality again and the magic would be lost.

I took the bus to High Street, and got off near a small, light brick building that was ominously plain against the deep blue and orange hues of the late afternoon sky. There were two doors. One said, Suite A Dr. Black, DDS. The other door said nothing more than Suite B. I walked in.

The office was small. There were only a few chairs, a table and a wooden broom—the sort marketed as "country decor" at craft stores around the start of autumn. I called out, asking if anyone was here. There was no response, but I could hear the rustling of papers in another room. The lightness was still here, the hope.

As I looked around for a sign-in sheet or some such thing, a round, bald head, shiny in the dim light, stuck out from the back doorway. When I said hello, the head retreated and more papers rustled.

"I'm closed. I forgot to lock the door," the man said in a sing-song voice.

"Oh. Can I make an appointment, then?"

"No appointments for a first meeting. People never show for first appointments. Walk-ins only."

"Okay. What are your hours?" I asked.

"That depends," he sang. "My wife is waiting, please come back another day."

The bus home wasn't due for ten minutes, and it was beginning to get cold outside. I looked around again, expecting maybe to notice something I had missed. "What's the broom for?" I asked.

He stepped out. His body was as round and buoyant as his voice, and he didn't seem irritated by my move to stall him. In fact, the question seemed to intrigue him. He walked up to me, and I noticed that he was almost my same height, 5'2", and this made me feel comfortable with him.

"This," he said, picking up the broom, "is for bad energies. For sweeping them away and starting again."

"Sir, I promise, you let me make an appointment, I'll show."

"Pushy, pushy," he said, nodding at my incorrigibility. "One minute. I'll give you that much. Now, sit. Tell me why you're here." I squatted slowly into a narrow wooden chair and eyed the broom, wondering if I would be swept.

"I've lost my memory. I forget everything."

He walked around me, then crouched down and examined my pupils. His were milky, like marbled blue taffy. He took his time. "Perhaps your memory is best not found?" he suggested.

"Perhaps," I said quickly, "but I need to find it if I'm going to keep my job."

He lifted my arm, told me to relax, and then released it. I held it there a moment before allowing the arm to fall. Next, he cradled my head in his warm, thick hands and rolled it to the side. "Have you been to a psychologist?"

"Yes. And a hypnotherapist, a neurologist... Nothing! They found nothing." I cringed at the desperation in my own voice.

The Healer looked me over the way men used to when I used to pay attention to such things. He stared for an uncomfortably long time; as though he were stunned by something he saw, and I knew I wasn't looking too attractive after nine hours at the blood bank, so I figured he was probably a freak, this was all an act. Just as I was about to stand up and walk out, he pulled back slightly. I waited for him to speak, but before I knew it, he hauled back and smacked me hard, across the face.

I froze. "What the fuck are you doing?" I yelled, too stunned to move. The man didn't frighten me, but something, perhaps a desire to believe, kept me from moving or retaliating. Men had swung at me before, men and women, and I wasn't one to cry over it—I swung back. But this was different. I felt no rage, only confusion. Just as the sting began to settle across my cheek, the back of his hand caught my other cheek. This time I stood. When I spoke next, I sounded like a child: "Why did you smack me?"

"Levity. You are dying, ready to join God." He backed a few more steps from me, as though he might catch something if I got too close now.

"Oh! So, you smack people then tell them they're dying. No wonder people don't show up to your appointments, you crazy fucker." I still sounded like a child. I attempted to compose myself, and asked, calmly, "Why would you smack a dying woman?"

"I smacked you to help you feel. You feel, right? The adrenaline. It's the most you've felt in weeks, right? I smacked you to remind you what life feels like, so there: diagnosis, cure. Enjoy your day." He reached for a small black backpack and flipped a light switch.

I hurried out, saying he was truly insane if he thought I'd pay him for that. And he called after me, amused: "It is okay, on the house." I turned, glared. His puffy face became thinner, as if he was sucking in his breath and holding it.

"You're a disturbed man," I yelled.

A bus had just stopped across the street; and as I ran to catch it. I realized how right the healer had been. I felt a jolt of adrenaline once more as the horn of a car honked and a heavy, wide sedan, light-blue and moving too quickly to stop in time, caught my foot and pushed me to the ground. Tires swelled above my unfeeling body and I honestly couldn't remember how to be afraid. I was thankful, as my life became something else.

Always a Story

I can't bring myself to visit Grandpa Homer in nearby Toledo, but I do what I can. I clean my mother's house. Meanwhile, I've learned that when Grandpa is frustrated at being unable to move, he yells at my grandmother, who yells at my mother. The residue of the yelling sticks to Mom, so to lessen it, I make her house look nice. I'm there to listen.

Rain taps away at the roof as I wait on Mom's porch. She's a little later than usual, but looks luminous when she arrives. She hugs me, cups my face in her hands, and says, "Thank you for being here." I follow her inside and wait for the story — there's always a story.

"Yesterday," she begins, with a touch of drama, "I had a spiritual experience with a bird."

"Mom, you're not on anything, are you?

"Sit, sit. Listen."

The phone rings and Mom rushes to answer it. I'm left thinking about the last time I hugged Grandpa Homer and how his skin was cool to the touch.

"Sorry, Sweetie. Okay, so I was taking out your grandparents' trash, and there he was — a peregrine falcon this big." She extends her arms to show me. "You know the type of bird I have as my screen saver?"

"Strange. Are they rare?"

Mom raises her hand, and a soft clang from her silver rings tells me to stop talking.

"Just listen. So, this bird lifts one wing, and I notice that the other one isn't moving. I step closer and see that it's injured. I start to talk to him. I say, 'It'll all be okay, Buddy, just stay right there,' and then I run into the house and call the zoo. I say there is a peregrine falcon outside my parents' house. A woman says I must be mistaken. I say no, I'm not, I have one as my screen saver, and she says, 'Yeah, whatever,' but that she'll send someone to the house."

"Was she rude to you?"

"That's not the point. Listen. So, I go back outside and tell the bird he'll be okay. Eventually, a Toledo Zoo van rolls up. A little bald guy gets out, looks past me, and says, 'Holy shit! That *is* a peregrine falcon!' I say,

'I told you!' He gets this huge carrier and begins gently nudging the bird, at its back end, until it's inside."

"Did the bird fight?"

"The bird went halfway inside. Then Bill, that was the man's name, told me that I could pet if I wanted. I put my hand on feathers, soft as flower petals, and he whipped his head around, fastlike. This stopped me; I got scared. His eyes were the color of fire—a burning orange, brighter than these walls. Then, before I could pull my hand away, he nestled his head in those giant black feathers and watched me pet him."

"Wow. That's a great story," I say.

Mom raises her hand to quiet me and then goes on. "Okay, so I start chatting this Bill up, you know how I do. And it turns out he was a Boy Scout, just like your Grandpa Homer. So, when the bird is safely in his carrier, I ask if Bill wouldn't mind showing the bird to Dad, and he agreed. We took the bird inside. Jen, I swear, color filled your grandpa's face. He said he knew exactly what kind of bird it was and he started talking about the Scouts. Bill said he was in the Scouts too, and the two of them started talking. The bird brought life into that room, I tell you. It only lasted for a short time, of course, and then your grandfather fell back into his state. But before leaving, Bill turned to me and said I could name the bird if I wanted."

"Did you name him Homer?"

"We went with your grandfather's middle name. Bill said he would try and fix the wing and release the bird back into the wild."

After dinner, I sit in front of my mother's computer. I stare at the picture of the falcon, trying to remember Grandpa Homer's middle name. I wonder if the bird's wing will heal. I wonder if Grandpa is comfortable.

"Are you staying the night?" Mom asks.

"No, I'll be leaving soon. I'll lock up."

Mom had stopped asking me to accompany her on trips to Toledo, so when I ask if she wants me to go with her next weekend, she hesitates for a moment. Sleepily, she says, "It'll be nice to have the company." She thinks I'll back out, I can tell, and I want to tell her I won't. I want to convince her, but she turns off the hallway light and disappears into her bedroom before I find the words. I watch the orange-rimmed eyes on the screen saver and I picture my grandfather: the icy texture of his hands, the small space his body occupies. I wonder what it was, exactly, that kept me away. This wonderment remains, long after the picture fades and the screen goes dark.

Composure

I had enough money to take a cab from O'Hare, but I decided to savor my arrival in Chicago. It was a city that made my hometown in Ohio seem postcard-still. I was seduced by the headiness, and I relished the rushed intensity. I checked my map and decided to take the shuttle to a bus stop at 10th Street, two miles from my aunt's apartment.

The address was printed on a tall pillar that separated two gates. I put my bag down a moment so that I could roll my shoulders and neck and tried to decode the smudged number I'd written on my forearm that morning. After a few tries, a gate swung open to reveal dozens of identical beige brick buildings. Unlike my own apartment complex, I didn't feel a thickness of silence and predictability, and I liked the fact that I didn't see any familiar faces. People sat on porches, talking and drinking cans of beer and soda. Cars thumped and roamed the parking lots, pausing in front of doors to honk or wave. Kids chased each other around a small courtyard that I passed just before reaching my aunt's door.

"This cannot be little Charlie," Claire said, greeting me with a tight hug. I collapsed into her embrace and then I collapsed onto her couch. I watched her move swiftly around her kitchen, which looked more like a hallway than an actual kitchen, and I told her how excited I had been to be in a big city. She laughed when I told her I took the long way and she told me to brace myself, that she'd show me the entire city that summer. Claire was more beautiful than I remembered, her eyes were the color of wet clay and with her small, plump mouth, she kissed me on each cheek and handed me a peanut butter sandwich with the crusts cut off, just like I used to eat them when I was a little kid.

***

I had been looking forward to my summer with Aunt Claire while Mom was in Massachusetts on some writing fellowship. My mother had been starting books for years, but this was the first one that, she said, showed real promise. The fellowship would allow her to finish the manuscript in its entirety, which was to be a short story collection, tentatively titled "Fledgling," that traced the lives of three separate women through painful and often comical break-ups. I was sick of reading my mother's drafts of the same stories rewritten with slightly varied characters. She produced these morbid, self-indulgent pieces since her divorce from my father, and I deplored them because I would always appear in the pages. Sometimes a woman's daughter, sometimes a son, I always found myself portrayed as the angsty kid, worrying over her or his father's absence. Sure, I was a little angsty, but hardly a worrier.

Claire's divorce had been more recent than my mother's, and she impressed me by the way she lacked all the self-pity Mom hoarded on the page. Both sisters' husbands had left them for other women but my father left us everything, and he sent me gifts on holidays. Claire, on the other hand, had lost her home, her car, even her dog, and had to borrow money from Mom just to pay her portion of the legal fees. She had no children, which had been, according to Mom, part of the reason her husband left her. She was, unlike my mother, a gentle, quiet woman, not easily shaken. When my own father left, years before, my mother locked herself in her bedroom and refused to write or do any other kind of work for months. Mother lived in slow-motion, then, walked through her depression as though it were a thick fog, and I had half-expected the loss would break my aunt down to the same state of inertia.

Claire must have sensed my worry because she was eager to show me just how composed she was. She spoke about her new approach to life, including her strict personal improvement regime that she had begun since she declared her independence. It included a raw food diet, daily exercise, and a daily affirmation that she said I should join her in reciting. "My life is a result of my own actions, and I choose only those actions that fulfill the best in me." She would recite these simple words to herself ten times each morning as she applied a myriad of brown eye shadows and coiled her auburn hair around her fingers until her curls resembled perfect little springs.

I tried the mantra once, but the seriousness of my aunt's face in the mirror next to mine caused me to chuckle. When I looked at my own eyes in the mirror, green and too small, in desperate need of some shadows or liners, I saw a kid laughing. I quickly apologized to her, realizing how immature I was being. But my aunt only joined in my laughter before pushing me out, saying she understood the silliness of it, but that no one could deny that what she was doing worked for her. "You'll understand one day. We all have a few tough chapters in our lives, and they only pass if you take control of your emotions. I want you to remember that, Charlie, and when you're going through a tough time. You just might benefit from your own mantra one day." She didn't say it as though it were a condemnation, my mother's trademark outlook on the woes of life, just as a matter of a fact.

I felt compelled to help my aunt. I took up most of the chores so that when she came home from her secretarial job, she could exercise or relax, whatever she wanted. I enjoyed spending time with her, in her small apartment, which seemed alive outside and cozy indoors. We often went out together on weekends, to the movies and out for dinner at exotic restaurants. Claire introduced me to sushi, caviar and seaweed. I've also tried buffalo and snake meat, and of course, everything soy that Claire shared off her own plates—this is a lot for a girl used to hot dogs and Hot Pockets. I even drank my first Mojito, which I savored, allowing each tingling sip to settle in my mouth until it lost its bite.

***

Claire's excessive cinnamon consumption left stains on her silverware that resembled rust, the sort of stains I had to really scrub to remove. Claire went through a jar of cinnamon in two weeks because she'd read that a teaspoon a day helps the body metabolize sugars. She didn't eat hardly anything sugary: no white bread, no milk, juice or soda; but even with her strict diet, she was always conscious of her weight.

I was scrubbing a fork clean, waiting for Claire to arrive home from work, when I heard the rumbling of talk radio with the bass turned up too high. I peered through the slatted blinds and saw a sun faded blue truck back into the parking space in front of the apartment. A solidly built man with curly brown hair and over-grown goatee slid out of the truck and stretched. His shirt lifted, exposing the brown hair on his rounded stomach. He spit into the grass that separated our porch from the parking lot.

I could see a woman in the passenger seat, but she didn't move. The man grabbed a battered cardboard box from the truck bed and yelled something at her in a gruff, demanding voice. The woman was heavy, almost twice his size, but she seemed somehow small next to him. He handed her a smaller box and the two made their way up creaking metal stairs, to the vacant apartment directly above Aunt Claire's. I could hear the ceiling creaking as they continued moving their belongings, and had his tone been a little softer with his partner, I probably would've offered to help, but he continued to bark at her, "Can't you carry more than that, I mean really, you're wasting trips. This'll take us all day." Intuition told me to stay my ass in the house until they were done.

The new neighbors got drunk that night, and as Claire and I tried to watch, How I Met Your Mother, a favorite of ours, we could hear the man above us yelling and slurring, and every now and then his wife laughing. Claire introduced herself to the man the next day, and he smiled flirtatiously, said something mildly offensive about how she shouldn't introduce herself to his girlfriend, that the 'old woman' might get jealous. My jaw grew tight as he spoke, and I noticed that he never even looked my way or asked my name. Even when Claire introduced me and he said hello, his eyes didn't waver from her.

The drunken noise from above us only got worse as days passed. What's more, although we rarely saw the woman, the man was always outside, yelling about something, either over the phone or to his wife inside. He would chain smoke or stand out on the balcony of the upstairs apartment, stomping furiously on soda cans until, I imagined, they were wafer flat, as we sat below on the porch, trying to read or talk. Instead of complaining, Claire would simply take her book inside and tell me how wonderful it would be when she saved up enough money to move into a bigger place. "There's talk that I'll get full-time work soon," she would say, "and that will really help out."

"Then you can get an apartment that isn't below those assholes," I said, pointing up.

I was afraid of the man that lived upstairs. I knew that his loudness was purposeful, disrespectful, even, and I didn't like the way that he never looked me up and down when we passed each other in the parking lot. He rarely spoke to either of us now, but when he did it was to Claire.

He would stand too close to her and complain about one of our other neighbors who had parked in his spot—there were no assigned spots—or left laundry in the dryer. On the first of the month I went to drop off the rent check for Claire. I walked into a small office with maroon walls and was greeted by a woman in a maroon suit, who looked about the same age as my aunt. She told me that she knew of my temporary stay, and that I was more than welcome to use the pool—I'd just have to ask her to let me in. As she spoke, I noticed that some of her lipstick had worked its way onto her teeth and I was busy wondering whether I should point it out, when she asked me to pass along a message to Claire. "One of your neighbors has been complaining about your alarm clock, that it's too loud and wakes him up every day." He'd also told the woman that he worked third shift and five in morning was his bedtime, the only time he really had to sleep. When I assured her that we would apologize to him, my voice must have portrayed a hint of sarcasm because she waved off the thought. "No, no. Technically, I am not at liberty to tell you who made the complaint because these things can turn confrontational. I just wanted you ladies to be aware." She told me that they weren't taking the complaint too seriously because the same neighbor had complained about many of the residents for equally silly things. But that we'd be wise to avoid the snooze button.

I wanted her to know I knew who it was, but not outright say so, so I told her about the stomping from the upstairs apartment, the way the man would sweep dirt and cigarette butts down on us, onto our porch, and how he would yell drunkenly at his wife late into the night. "You know, the time when he says he's working." She nodded knowingly and said she had heard such things from others and that she doubted the two would be around long.

Furious, I ran home to Claire and told her about the complaint. She told me not to worry, that it was no big deal to avoid the snooze button. It was one of her bad habits anyway.

"But he's the loud neighbor. He's the one that keeps us up at night and drops all that trash onto our porch."

"I'm sure he doesn't mean to bother us. I'll go talk with him. I feel bad that we've never even had coffee with the two of them."

"Those people are alcoholic trash," I said. Claire looked disapproving. I went on, "I mean, I get bad vibes from them. I don't think it'd be a good idea."

"You have a little growing up to do," she said. "It'd be nice if you'd come along. Adults don't have the time to be petty and judgmental." We heard stomping above us and we both gazed up at the pocked ceiling. "You know what? I changed my mind. I'll go by myself. You mind starting a load of laundry?"

"Maybe you shouldn't go. I mean, really, that guy creeps me out."

Claire waved off my comment and hustled up the aching metal stairs. I heard her knock on the door, and I walked out onto the porch, hoping their screen door was open and I could hear what she'd say. I heard nothing. In fact, it was the quietest that apartment had been since the couple had moved in.

Too much time had passed, and I was getting nervous. Busy pacing, I forgot about the laundry and busied myself with ideas about what must be going on upstairs. I imagined the couple's reaction to my soft-voiced aunt. "What, you think you're better than us?" the man would ask. The woman would back her husband up, "Yeah, you think you're better than us?" Then she'd eye my aunt's perfectly sculpted body, and add, "Skinny bitch!"

Just as I was about to run up after Claire, she opened the door. "They said they'd keep it down," she said with a smile. "And that they never thought twice about sweeping the balcony or how loud it was to crush cans. They said that, like me, they had moved from a house, and were used to having their own space. So see? A misunderstanding." She sighed, motioning toward the laundry I'd forgotten.

Later that night, when the stomping began, I saw every bit of my mother in Claire's tightly-clenched mouth. It was the look my mother got for much more benign things. She gave it to clerks when they accidently rang up a grocery item twice or a waiter had forgotten, for the second time, that she'd asked for a glass of ice water. It was a look that preceded arguing and, usually, a free item or meal. From my aunt, I didn't know what it would precede, but I knew they were finally getting to her. She continued to look irritated throughout the week as a series of loud stomps that lasted for minutes at a time woke us up throughout the night, accompanied by yells of, "I sure hope we're not being too loud for the neighbors." And "Wouldn't want to disturb someone's beauty rest." The yelling was all him, but I could tell his wife was joining in on the stomping. It was a mutual effort, and I wondered whether she was joining in to satisfy him or whether she really was jealous of Claire.

It wouldn't matter in the end. Like Claire's ex-husband, the man who lived above us ultimately kicked his wife out on the street. We saw the fight pique in the parking lot. We huddled on Claire's bed, peering out of the blinds. Someone had called the police. The man seemed eerily calm, just smiling and acting surprisingly cordial when the police arrived.

"What the hell happened there?" Claire asked me. We began to speculate. Maybe none of it was real. Maybe the two of them were really independently wealthy, sociologists who were trying to judge the effects of irritating behaviors on neighbors so that they could write a book on how much people could actually take. We said they might be method actors. "Haven't you noticed the woman looks a bit like Scarlett Johansen—if she gained two hundred pounds?" I said. She said, "Drug smugglers; circus people, who were practicing at home; depressed evangelists, exposed for corruption years ago and still working to re-establish their church." We went back and forth like this for too long, but it was fun making up these stories until we both caught ourselves laughing and paused long enough to watch the woman sob. Things stop being funny quickly sometimes.

The man, whose goatee was now shaven, looked satisfied and the woman, no longer his partner in crime but someone who deserved our sympathy, looked as though her life were over now. Her cheeks glistened, highlighted by the blue and red lights of the car, and for a brief moment she looked directly at Claire and me. Neither of us averted our eyes. There was no threat there. Then, when he turned around, we backed away from the blinds. Although things didn't quiet down after that day, we never saw the woman again.

***

When I returned home in August, Mom was cheery. She said the writer's retreat was energizing, just what she needed. Claire had recently purchased a car, thanks to full-time work and a little alimony check that her ex-husband had been court-ordered to pay. Even with Mom's new upbeat mood, I missed Claire, our talks, and outings. Things went back to normal, me in Dayton, walking a little quicker than everyone else, going to the same restaurants after school with my friends, hearing the same gossip, seeing the same low-energy downtown crowds at the city mall.

It was almost October when Mom told me Claire had gone missing. As soon as I heard the news, the neighbor's face popped into my mind; it was an unconscious association, like the thought of marshmallows and chocolate with graham crackers. I stopped eating. I missed all the news, watching only reruns of Golden Girls and Mash from my bed. Turns out, I had come down with a respiratory infection around the same time that we were notified of Claire's disappearance. Mom said stress exacerbated my condition and it was a good thing that I was getting rest.

I was able to stomach soups and honey-thickened teas by the time I got the news. I was reading one of Mom's manuscripts when she entered my room with a stark, fearful look on her face. "What's going on?" I asked. She sat at the edge of my bed and my stomach sank. "Is it about Claire?"

Mom only looked away. I begged her to tell me what she knew, said I could handle it. The stories in my head had to be worse than the truth. I imagined that asshole neighbor of hers had murdered her after she'd accidentally hit the snooze button one morning. Maybe he'd raped her and then murdered her; maybe his wife had returned and murdered both of them... "Please, Mom. I need to know." My mother, a self-proclaimed woman of words, refused to speak. But, she had news. She stroked my forehead and told me to brace my sick little self. She said, "Now we don't know everything, but this article will explain better than I can right now." I read:

Sheila Jones, girlfriend of Doug Jansen and recent inmate of Ross Correctional Facility, entered her apartment at 1353 Olmos Street at approximately 8PM to find him dead, stabbed twenty times. Neighbors reported sounds of yelling and struggle, and eyewitnesses said that Claire Richards had entered his apartment shortly before the yelling began. Doug Jansen died at approximately 8:13PM. Sheila Jones was arrested but soon acquitted when fingerprints on the knife were traced back to Claire Richards. She is still at large.

When questioned why he didn't report the yelling, one resident of the Olmos Apartment Complex reported that he was used to hearing Doug yell, and thought little of it. It was the quiet that should have tipped him off.

My mother held me for a long time that night as I sobbed like a child, not so much for the loss of life as for the loss of what I emulated in my aunt. And as my mother brushed a sweaty strand of my hair from my forehead I asked her not to write about Claire, not to reduce her to what the rest of the world would. Her face grew solemn as she refused, saying that I was asking her to do the one thing she couldn't promise; I was wrong for asking, she said. I'd understand one day.

Claire was arrested shortly after the story appeared. I accepted the charges when she called from prison. She told me where she was, how long she'd be there—probably the rest of her life—and said that she was in a cell with a woman who had raped her own son. She spoke breezily about her cellmate, saying the woman was a remarkable chess player, and really quite nice.

The first and last time I went to visit my aunt, I didn't know what or how to feel. In fact, it was like I had no feeling at all about the situation, or perhaps I had so many feelings that they'd all somehow combined to create a sort of numbing effect. I spoke to her over the phone, watching her through a murky plastic wall, and when I reached out my hand to touch the plastic she just smiled. Claire said very little, but when she spoke she smiled. She told me I'd grown quite a bit; that she'd read my mother's novel and that she loved us both very much. I asked her if she was sorry for what she'd done. I watched her chest rise and fall, and I thought about how beautiful she was as I waited for her to cry out in remorse. "Regret is an emotion that won't help anyone or anything," she said. "I have to think positively." I listened to her recite what I figured to be a new mantra, and I wanted so desperately to help her feel things the way my mother did. As she began talking about her routine inside, the books she planned to read and the exercise regime she'd made for herself, I waited for her to breakdown. I wanted a show—pain, self-wallowing, regret, anger, anything. But she was too busy coping to reflect.

Asleep

Over the summer I slept, eight hours most nights and two-three hours during the day. When I wasn't asleep, I might as well have been. A doctor friend of mine, who I hadn't heard from in a while, invited me to drinks and I told him all about it. He said that my low energy was a classic symptom of depression, to which I said that depression is a mainstay in everyone's life, coming and going, and I didn't think the term was precise enough. He toasted my insight, then confided that he was depressed in the most classic and generic manner possible. Given the opportunity, he said, he planned to do something exciting to distract himself from his feelings. He said that when he felt low, energetic distraction was more beneficial than sleep, and that he'd been mulling over the possibility of having an affair. I nodded, thinking it might work temporarily. Or, maybe, he said, he'd take a vacation—somewhere unusual and exciting—or he'd buy a new car. Jokingly, I suggested he go for the affair, explaining that it'd likely be far cheaper than the alternatives. We toasted to this, too, and I felt quite clever until the doctor leaned in and tried to kiss me. I turned my head, and as his lips brushed my chin, took a sip of my martini.

***

My months of hypersomnia had been rather nice and, I quickly began to believe, quite necessary. It was as though my body knew the stress looming and had simply been preparing. Autumn arrived like an alarm, and I awoke to chaos. My mother called and said she had been diagnosed with mercury poisoning. After making the arrangements to fly her to New Mexico to stay with me, I realized that my home was nowhere near ready for company. My summer vacation from teaching was almost at a close and I had syllabi to make and students' names to memorize. I thought about how consuming my mother could be as I cleaned and made lists of items I would have to buy to ensure her comfort. She's a lovely woman, but my father, when he was alive, spoiled her beyond repair. I knew I would have to maintain his standard or else I would be subjected to her over-developed ability to whine and bitch: sheets must have a minimum number of threads, air must be ionized, almond milk and Sumatra must be readily available in the kitchen at all times. My mother would insist upon fresh flowers in her bedroom and a precise amount of lighting that I would not be able to deliver until she arrived to tell me. My mother would also likely tell me what to wear, and this led to my volunteering at the college for early morning classes so that she couldn't catch me before I left for work. I had it all planned out. The arrangement would be temporary, the right thing, and I would be fulfilling my duty as a responsible daughter.

The doctor called me while I was sitting in a row of uncomfortable plastic chairs, watching travelers search for luggage on an over-loaded belt of identical black and dark blue baggage. He apologized for the discomfort he may have caused that weekend when he'd gone in for a kiss. He said he was embarrassed, couldn't stop thinking about it, and that he didn't want our friendship to end on his blunder. I told him not to worry. "You're a beautiful woman," he said, "and I just couldn't see anything else that night." I told him it was fine, just fine, and that if he wanted to make it up to me, he could subject himself to a dinner with my mother tomorrow, at my house. I invited Frances, his wife, and he said they'd be there. Seven o'clock; they were to bring wine.

My mother rolled out in a wheelchair, which she quickly admitted had been quite unnecessary, but it got her off the plane quicker, so why not? She handed me a large purse she'd had resting on her lap and explained that she'd chosen to have her items shipped and they'd be arriving within a few days. "I might have to buy a few new things, but as weak as I feel lately, shopping is about the only thing that will keep me out of bed anyway. Now, honey, I'm not going to be burdensome. I want you to know that your help is appreciated. Your sister didn't even offer to drive me to the airport, let alone ask me to stay with her. This is why you've always been my favorite. You're the responsible one. We've always been able to count on you."

"How is Janice?" I asked.

"She's fine. Travels a lot. We don't speak much anymore, now that she's got that girlfriend of hers. I swear, the girl thinks she's doing something new by becoming a lesbian. It's almost as though she's too good for us now."

I hadn't known my sister was a lesbian, but the news was tepid at best. I hadn't spoken to Janice in three years, and then it had been at my father's funeral. She'd always been rebellious toward my parents, blaming them for everything wrong in her life, and I simply didn't have the patience for it. "I hope that coming out will put the girl in a better mood," I said.

My mother laughed. Her sticky, red lipstick had spread to her teeth and when I pointed this out she grew quiet again. "I've arranged a sort of homecoming dinner tomorrow. A few of my friends will be over. Are you up for that?" I asked.

"Oh, dear, of course. I'd love to meet some of your friends here. I can't wait to see your home." She clasped her hands together and then leaned into me a bit. "I've missed you, darling. Do you have a cig?"

"I quit, Mom."

"Good for you. It's a nasty habit, stains the teeth, and nowadays it even angers people when you light up. I assume here in New Mexico things are a bit more laid back?"

"A bit."

My mother did look sick, smaller than I remembered her being and skinnier than me. I went to put my arm around her and she stopped me, told me to hang on, maybe go get the car. She eased up to a man in a cowboy hat and flirtatiously asked him for a cigarette. I called out that I'd bring the car around. She waved and nodded and then returned her gaze to the man, who I have no doubt, she wanted to bed. By the time I retrieved the car and drove around to where she stood, she was wearing the cowboy hat and laughing. As I honked, she handed the man, who was tall and solidly built, her business card before walking slowly toward me. My mother was in the real estate business up north, so there was no practical reason to give this man her card, unless he happened to be moving soon. "Mom, he was my age," I said, hearing the childlike tone to my voice.

"He's a man who is just beginning to bald, who writes poetry, and he's a land monger, a savvy investor. He owns quite a bit of real estate. But he's been all business his whole life. The man has no social life. I'll be good for him. Besides, he said he was forty. He's got ten years on you, kid."

"Mom, are you really sick?" My mother didn't speak to me the rest of the night, except to thank me for showing her to her room and to ask that I leave her to rest a while.

The next day, as it always happened with my mother, all was forgiven. The cowboy had been invited to my mother's homecoming dinner and he would be arriving at seven. She asked me if I had enough food, and offered to pay for whatever I would need to buy if not. "I'm ordering in," I said. "It's a nice place though, and they always bring too much food. You know, Mom, you should've asked me before you invited the cowboy over to dinner, you don't even know him."

"No man that offers an old woman his hat upon first meeting is all bad," she said.

The doctor showed up before the cowboy, but his wife was not with him. When I answered the door, I had on a long crème colored dress with embroidered flowers at the bottom. It had been a dress my mother picked from my closet, and I felt awkward in it, over-dressed.

"Wow," he said. "You keep looking so beautiful, and it'll be hard for me to keep from another awkward moment."

"Where's Frances?" I asked.

"She didn't feel up to going out. She insisted I come alone," he said. 'I think she's having an affair; he's probably already there, sticking it in as we speak." My mouth dropped, not at the comment, but his complete disregard for the fact that my elderly mother was somewhere inside, very likely eavesdropping. I shushed him, and he handed me a bottle of wine and a container. "I made tiramisu, spent hours on it, so even if it's horrible, I'd be obliged if you'd take a bite."

"You first," I said. I motioned for him to enter, asking him to check his sexual references at the door, and told him to go find a seat in the kitchen where I could see my tiny, red-haired mother sitting with her tumbler of Bailey's.

"I completely forgot your mother was here," he said, to which I cut my eyes at him.

After a fast-friendship was made between my mother and the doctor, the cowboy arrived. He wore a new, darker hat that resembled the one he'd given my mother, and matching boots, which he wiped off feverishly before entering my home. "I brought you a few candles," he said. "My sister said that candles make good housewarming presents."

"Um, thanks. I don't think we've properly met, I'm Candice."

"Jim," he said, extending his hand. "Where's that beautiful mother of yours?" I motioned toward the kitchen and stood in the foyer a moment, collecting myself.

Briefly, I wished for my solitary summer days, days full of sleep and less company, as I watched the cowboy sidle into my kitchen and join the doctor and my mother, who were now laughing voraciously. I also wondered, briefly, why my mother didn't act sick. She looked weak, but her energy seemed high. Perhaps she was on the mend after all, and she'd exaggerated her need for rest. Or maybe, like mine, her body just needed the extra rest to balance itself out from what had happened or was to come.

The dinner went remarkably well, and my mother kept both men riveted with her spirited discourse on the evil nature of the diet industry and how they were to blame for her sickness. "I was told to eat salmon and no red meat, and I took that advice to heart. I ate salmon every day, and now look at me, I can't even work. At sixty-three, I'm already a burden on my poor daughter." My mother did hit a sort of wall after a few hours and had to excuse herself to lie down. This left me to entertain the cowboy and doctor, which I wasn't up to doing.

"Candice, your mother is something else," the doctor said. The cowboy clapped his hand and agreed. He confided to us that my mother had asked him out on another date and that he was considering it.

"I've never been with an older woman in my life, but that mother of yours." The men laughed. The doctor said something about what a woman that age could teach a young man and I punched him on the arm. "You all have been quite entertaining, but it's time you leave my house," I said in a playful tone. They both collected their things, but after the cowboy left, I asked the doctor if he could help me clean up a little to which he gave me a sinister smile that, I admit, made my stomach tingle. I wanted him to kiss me again, and so as we cleared plates, I gave him the opportunity, stood close, reached over him. The smile didn't leave his face; he didn't try anything. "You're a good daughter," he said.

"You're a good friend."

"You're feeling better?" he asked.

I nodded, asked, "You?"

"Right now I am." The doctor was tall, at least a foot taller than me, and as we stood together, rinsing dishes and piling them into the dishwasher, I entertained the thought of sleeping with him for the first time since we met. As soon as I thought it, though, thoughts of Frances arrived and overshadowed my desire. I imagined her, not one of my best friends, but a friend nonetheless, weeping into her pillow as her husband sheepishly admits to his affair. I imagine the doctor lying to her for months and the tension between them growing until it becomes unbearable. I imagine our friendship ending, and the occasional weekend drink that I've taken for granted these past three years, the fun conversation and dry humor we share, coming to an end. And I decide that this is only temporary. If my mother can find a cowboy, twenty years her junior, at the airport, I can find a suitable partner, one that didn't come with so much potential loss.

The doctor closed the dishwasher quietly and shoved the three wine bottles the four of us had emptied into a corner on the counter before wiping it off. "Thank you," I said to my friend. He cupped my chin and said you're welcome.

My mother was asleep by the time the doctor left. I didn't sleep that night. The next morning, however, she couldn't shut up about how perfect we'd be for each other. "He's handsome, a little ornery. Just like you. It's perfect."

"Mom, he's married," I said. 'How are you feeling anyway, you kind of crashed on us last night."

"I'm just fine. I'm actually beginning to think that you brought me back to life, chickie. The doctors said I'd be out of commission for months, but I feel fine, even after all that traveling and whatnot. I wasn't any more tired than I wouldn't have been without this mercury in my blood. Now listen, Candice, you shouldn't date a married man."

"I know, Mom, that's what I just said."

"But that man is going to leave his wife. I can just tell—you know your mother knows these things. So listen, you tell him you'll be with him when he leaves his wife, and presto, a little waiting, she'll be out of the picture. I can tell... I can tell by the way he looks at you. And you know I believe in the sanctity of marriage. I never once cheated on your father, and boy did I want to a few times. But I'm telling you, I feel it in my gut, girlie. He's the one." I stared at my mother for a long time and she stared back. I didn't want to be the first to break our mutual gaze and so I searched her eyes for more explanation. "He's the one," she conceded.

"Fuck," I said under my breath, "Fuck, fuck, fuck."

"Call him tonight. Tell him," she went on. She was like that little devil that sits on your shoulder and tells you to do what you know will get you in trouble. She was like a dealer, a pimp, telling me what I needed to be happy, doling out the cure without any basis in reality, offering me a quick fix.

The high nasally tone of Frances's voice made my stomach drop. "Hello, Frances, it's Candice. Can I speak to your husband right quick?"

"Hello, Candice. How are you? Listen, I know you're mad. Robert told me you really wanted me to come and meet your mother, but I want you to know I was feeling antisocial last night. Don't know what it was, probably stress. This is always a stressful time in retail. Anyway, thanks for getting my husband drunk, girl, when he got home..." she raised her voice on the word home and I imagined Robert getting home and ravaging his wife as he thought of me. I imagined his naked body, his closed eyes, my lonely self in a bed at home, thinking of him as he thought of me.

"Anytime," I said. "Listen, I guess I really don't need to talk with Robert. Will you just tell him he left his dessert container? I can bring it by later, but I just wanted you all to know."

"Sure thing, sweetie."

That night my mother began to sweat and shake. As she talked to me her words became a jumbled, jagged line of sound. I drove her to the emergency room. She was admitted for observation and over the next few days, as her health wavered, the cowboy arrived and refused to leave her side. I returned to work. I had no interaction with Robert, but I thought about him often and wondered if he'd ever pick up his container. I spent a lot of time in the hospital, where I couldn't always get cell phone reception, and I wondered sometimes if he'd tried to call or stop by. Once in a while, I'd try his house, but it was always Frances who answered and I'd taken to hanging up the phone rather than talking to her. Her voice had a way of twisting my stomach, and as I held my mother's hand, on her first night back home, I confessed my feelings. "Oh honey, I'm sorry. I think you missed your chance." The cowboy spent the night with her that night, bringing her Earl Gray with almond milk and reading to her late into the night. I listened from the kitchen, where I sat up, unable to sleep, watching the phone.

As mother's strength returned, she announced her plans. Her doctors said that much of what had slowed her down was flushed from her body, and that she'd only get better from here. "And so, my dear, I'll be moving in with Jeff." The cowboy's name was Jeff, and I had been encouraged to begin calling him by his name. "After all, he just might be your stepfather one day."

"I don't want you to leave, Mom," I said, worrying she was rushing in with Jeff, worrying that she may grow ill again and I wouldn't know.

"No offense dear, but Jeff takes care of me in ways you can't."

After making a childish gagging sound, I dialed Robert's cell phone, which I wasn't supposed to call unless it was an emergency as he used it for work. When he answered, I didn't hear the lightness in his voice that I usually did. I figured it was because he was working or thought I was a patient, serious business. But when I told him it was me, his tone stayed flat. I told him we should get drinks sometimes and he said, simply, that he didn't think it was such a good idea.

"What happened?" I asked Mom through an endless stream of embarrassing and ridiculous tears, the kind of tears I hadn't known I was capable of shedding for a married man. Jeff had stopped over to check on Mom, and I had been so consumed, I'd forgotten he was there. He put his arm around me as Mom stroked my head.

"Sorry, Hon, you missed your window there. A mother just knows these things. Now, you'll just have to move on. You're the one that wanted to play things safe. It's a good thing, sweetie, you probably spared that woman a lot of pain, or at least bought her some time. You've always been responsible and I envy you that."

I was so relieved that Mom was better, happy that she'd found her cowboy, and perplexed at how she always seemed so vigorous, even at the height of her illness. "A body in motion stays in motion," she liked to say. As I helped my mother pack, I told Jeff how important fresh flowers were, almond milk, good coffee and that she could take the sheets I'd picked up for her those weeks ago. I stood in the doorway and waved as they pulled off, so filled with promise, probably planning out their mutual interest in real estate and what my mother would have to do to get licensed in the state. I felt as though I'd just given my mother away, and I blew a kiss at their truck as they pulled off. As I watched the gravel spit up from the back tires, I yawned. I will finish grading papers, I thought, and then settle in for a long nap. I will dream of what's to come.

D20-XC8

Sheila's thigh brushes against me as Antone rambles on about an ice bar he saw on The Food Channel. "We have to go. All the drinks are served in cups made of pure ice, and they make you wear a thermal suit while you're there. You're so numb, you just drink and drink. Then you go outside, thaw out, and realize you're, like, really fucked up."

At one time, I'd think such a place ridiculous, but since they've stationed me here in Florida in the middle of summer and since I'm now confined to a room with no ventilation and an overpopulation of over-sized insects, the ice bar doesn't sound so bad. Come to think of it, I long just to watch The Food Channel. When I used to work in Housewares at Wal-Mart, I found myself addicted to the channel, which was always on in the store. Purees and foams were popular when I last watched—a trend that disturbed me to no end.

Sheila's really leaning into me now. If only Antone knew. Last week, she visited me in a short summer dress, and without a word lifted it, rode me into the early hours—long before the cacophony of alarms began to sound through the thin apartment walls. She was inexhaustible that day, and eventually, reluctantly, I just stopped moving, unable to go even a second longer.

I still shudder when I think about it. And now, when Sheila gives me money to go, I can't. Her mood shifts and Antone begins to yell—like I care!—and then pound on me with his bony fists. I feel dents forming, and just when I feel I might come to life, I shut down completely, the electricity drains from my body. I hear him cursing our apartment complex, calling me dirty, a piece of shit, trying to pry his money from my insides. He'll never get it back.

As they walk out, with soggy clothes, I feel a jolt and begin to shake, slowly so they won't hear. Just when they're out of sight, the heat comes and I begin to really go, tumbling, nothing but air.

Untied

Nathan watches his wife dart around the kitchen. Eva rummages through the grocery bags that Nathan placed on the counter. She shoves food haphazardly into cupboards and refrigerator compartments. Her dark hair is pulled back in a twist. As she bundles the bags into a ball and crams them into a drawer with the others, she pauses a moment to look at him; her thickly-lined, over-shadowed eyes narrow as he takes a seat at the table. He responds with a warm smile, a subtle hand motion toward the phone angled between his ear and shoulder.

"Is she there?" Ginger asks.

"Yes, Ma'am."

Nathan knows that no woman would suspect her husband would speak to his mistress right in front of her, not when he could easily slip away to another room or wait until she's not around. He's being strategic, not overconfident.

"Nathan. What the hell?" Eva asks, reaching for one of the items on the counter, "is this?" She thrusts the object within an inch his face.

All Nathan can see is white. He shoves the object away from him and motions to the phone at his ear, this time with a more pronounced motion, including a pointed finger. He says, "Yes, yes, I'll pay the bill online today. Yes. I'm going to do it right now. And thank you." Nathan smiles, snaps the phone shut. "That was outright rude, dear. I was on the phone."

"What bill?" Eva asks.

"Credit card."

"You still haven't paid the credit card bill? What's wrong with you? And what's this? Why are these groceries just sitting here? I appreciate that you went shopping, but there's no point if the stuff is going to sit here and go bad."

"I just got home," Nathan says, "and the phone rang before I got a chance."

"I just got home, too, Nathan, so why am I unpacking the groceries? You could help with that fucking free hand you were using to point to the phone." Eva stands with her finger in the handle of a milk jug. "Let's try this again. What's this?"

"It's milk."

She grabs a glass and reaches in the cabinet for a jelly jar and pours an inch of vodka and then an inch of Kahlua. The two bottles are never far from her reach, he thinks as she stares him down, arms akimbo. "What?" he finally asks.

"Milk? 2% Milk? Are you trying to kill me?"

"It was on sale."

"You know I can't digest milk. You're trying to kill me, destroy my stomach? How the hell am I supposed to make cereal? How am I supposed to lighten my coffee? And how the hell am I supposed to make a White Russian without my soymilk? Kahlua and vodka is sick. Taste this shit." She shoves the jar of the thick brown liquid at him, pushing it under his nose.

"Don't drink then, if it's that big a deal."

"You really want to see me without a drink after work? Fine, you got it. Just wait till tomorrow, when I can't have my coffee either." Her self-directed dig is not meant to be funny, but he laughs nonetheless. "And what's this?" She looks in another bag as he waits. "You bought spaghetti sauce and no spaghetti? If you want to play the househusband, learn the fuck to shop like you have some sense. Buy things that go together, things we can consume without pain. Soy milk! Tuna! Spaghetti! Stuff we eat, not half-assed attempts at meals just because you can save a penny. You know, a penny doesn't count for anything if all our food goes bad. You know that right?"

"You're the one that gave me those coupons. I just bought what was on special. I thought you'd give me coupons for food we need."

"Nice effort, Nathan." Her rigid movements made her look somehow fragile, as though something as simple as soymilk or spaghetti was all she had to look forward to and he had ruined that, ruined her day by neglecting to complete this simple shopping trip to her satisfaction. He watches as she pops the cap off the milk carton and smells the liquid, scrunching up her nose.

"I'll drink the milk, Eva. Sam will drink the milk. Calm down. I'll go out and get soy first thing tomorrow morning, okay? Before you wake up, so you can have your coffee."

"Don't overexert yourself," Eva says. She takes her hair down and stretches her arms above her head, rolls her neck from side to side and takes a seat across from her husband and rests her head on the table. Her face looks worn as she stares at the drink she's poured.

Nathan assesses his wife's face. He's been watching her closely, monitoring the changes that had occurred since she'd turned thirty. Some women's beauty piques in their mid-thirties, as their skin loses the puffiness of youth and the cheekbones and natural lines seem only to magnify the features. Only Eva's eyes betray her, show her weariness. But at the same time, there's something almost sexy about her worn look—she begins to remind him of Mrs. Ramon, a perpetually-exhausted English professor whose bra strap would occasionally fall to her shoulder as she lectured about proper usage. Women, it seemed to Nathan, didn't cope well with hard work, and being a man who noticed this made him less sensitive to their moodiness. A tired woman, a woman who worked as hard as a man, needs to be ignored until he finds a way to rescue her and offer reprieve. He knew Eva would be all the more grateful, after a tough year, and that she'd been lying to him when she said she no longer desired sexual pleasure. Her desire was there, and when he found work again, was able to offer her reprieve, he'd unleash all that pent up sexuality and she'd be fiercer than ever in bed. For now, though, he has to make do in order to preserve his own sense of optimism. He has no choice but to sleep with Ginger, to satisfy his own needs until the job climate shifts and he can reclaim his role around here.

"You're beautiful," he says. "Relax. I'll finish with the groceries."

After a few seconds of silence, in which Nathan begins to finish the job, putting away the dry groceries Eva had left on the counter, she returns his appeal for peace. "Look, I'm just tired. Thanks for shopping, or thanks for trying, anyway. You have to start thinking things through."

"Are you two bickering?" Sam asks. Her use of the word bicker makes both husband and wife smile. Sam pushes herself from the doorway, sliding socks on linoleum toward her mother. She gives Eva a tight squeeze and spins around to reach for a bag of soft-chew cookies. "See, this is the kind I like. I can't stand the crunchy ones."

"See, I did one thing right," Nathan says, happy to have his daughter's approval. He pats the girl on her head and the two of them smile, conspiratorially, at Eva.

"This girl doesn't need cookies," Eva says. "Buy Sam granola bars or something. Have you seen her little pudgy tummy lately?"

"Hey, I'm not pudgy." She lifts her shirt and reconsiders. "Okay, a little, but you should be happy. Most of the girls at my school are anorexic. I think I look better than them."

"You're cute, honey, but there's a difference between healthy and pudgy."

"Hey!"

"Look, Mommy's tired and a little bitchy, but you need to wait until after dinner," Eva says, snatching the cookies from her daughter. "I'm going to rest with my nasty, half-assed, make-shift White Russian and I'll reemerge for dinner. Got that family?"

"Sam and I will make dinner," Nathan says. "You relax. And hey, you might like the drink; people drink it like that, you know. It's called a Black Russian."

"Just because there's a name for it… Oh never mind. I'm going to suffer through my 'Black Russian' on the couch, and if you love me at all, you'll both leave me alone." She takes a generous drink. "I'll give you this much," she says as she walks away, "it is stronger this way."

"Dad, am I pudgy?"

"A little, baby. But kids your age are pudgy. Don't worry about it."

"Dad? I won't be pudgy anymore if you buy me a bike, you know like Angel has? Have you seen her bike Dad? She's skinny and I bet it's because she has that bike. She rides it everywhere. It's purple. Her dad bought it for her for no reason. No birthday, nothing, just because he loves her. You should do that, Dad. I'm a good kid."

"You're all right," Nathan says, laughing, patting his girl on her pudgy stomach, "but you know we have money problems. Your Mom drinks up her salary —"

"Fuck you, Nathan, I do not!"

Nathan bends down to whisper. "And besides, Kiddo, I'm between jobs. It won't be long before I'm working again and can spoil you rotten. But for now, don't make it worse by always bringing up stuff we don't buy you. We'll buy you that bike soon enough."

"But Dad, I'll help pay. I have fourteen dollars in my room from Christmas."

"There's no such thing as a bicycle that costs fourteen dollars, Sam."

"Let's look. Maybe we can put a down payment on one like you did with the car."

"No."

"My precious, darling family," Eva shouts from the other room, "Shut up! I'm trying to take a nap."

Nathan hands his daughter a box of macaroni and cheese. "You make this, and I'll put on some burgers in a few. Sound good?"

The girl nods eagerly. "I'll make it my own way. Mac and cheese a la Sam."

"Go for it girl. I'll be right back. Get one of those tofu burgers out for your mother." He takes his phone to the back porch and dials Ginger's number. "Hey babe, sorry I had to hang up on you like that. She's in one of her moods."

"Come see me," she says.

"If only," Nathan says, watching from the window as Sam pours the package of small curled noodles into a pot of water. She stuffs another cookie in her mouth and then looks around for her mother before taking a second one and placing it in her jean skirt pocket.

"You know, Nathan, you better warn that wife of yours. I think I'm going to steal you away if she doesn't start treating you better."

"Don't tempt me now," he says as he imagines the impossible situation. Him, living in Ginger's huge beachfront home, leaving Eva with a mortgage she couldn't handle, leaving her with the promise to forever continue on in this tired, unrewarding cycle. He isn't tempted, but it comforts him to think of Eva in such a helpless state without him, if only she could see the situation from his angle.

The two of them have yet to make love, but Ginger caresses Nathan daily with assurances, and he knows that he can't resist her physically for much longer. Ginger's kindness, the presents she insists he take—grocery money, credit card payments and other small incidental items for the household, even the flowers he offers Eva occasionally—and the adoration she exudes without expecting a return, is exactly what his wife would offer if she didn't feel so depended upon. But he couldn't let her know that they were better off financially than they were because this would lead to questions. So he allows her to think the bills are always piling up, the flowers are always picked, he actually takes the time to look at and use the coupons that she gives him for groceries. The fact of the matter is, Nathan knows women, their fickle nature, and to count on Ginger would be a mistake. She's a temporary windfall that came along at just the right time, but no woman can be relied on for too long.

In the beginning, almost ten years ago now, it had been Eva's rough edges, the way she seemed so genuine, despite lacking the niceties and sometimes even the social etiquette, that seemed to distinguish her from other women. When Nathan's mother died, Eva had genuinely cared, and she listened when he confided that he was never close enough to his mother to love her. Despite the fact that he'd been beaten as a child, Nathan knew that a man could never say he didn't love his mother, not out loud, not to another woman. But Eva had understood. Like him, she'd been self-reliant. She'd left home at age sixteen and never looked back. Romantic interludes, Ginger's loans and niceties: these are only temporary. Their affair will be temporary, too. Meanwhile, the anticipation of it, he has to admit, is beginning to consume him.

"I should probably go," he says, picturing Ginger in a skirted business suit, opened to reveal a low cut shirt; she was packaged like this when they'd met and he couldn't see her in anything else when he pictured her. Her naked body was still a mystery, though he often imagined taking her in that very outfit, lifting her up on a chair and feeling his way beyond the skirt, making her scream as her legs wrapped around him—those spiky high heels still on her feet.

"You have no idea how much I want to see you right now," he says. He hears Sam let out a small yell and sees her wave her finger around and run some tap water over it.

"Shit. I think my daughter burned herself. I have to go again. I just wanted to apologize for getting off the phone the way I did. You understand, right baby? We'll see each other soon."

"I understand. Listen, I know we won't have time alone until Monday, but I'm having a yard sale Saturday. You should bring your daughter. Tell her you want to buy her something. Whatever you want, I'll give it to you. I know you don't want me to meet her, but this would be like a test run. She wouldn't know who I was, just see my face. I could see hers. I'm so curious about her."

"Yard sale? That doesn't sound like you," he says, noticing that his daughter has recovered like a champ. She's humming a Lady Gaga song that he wishes he didn't know the words to.

"Yeah, I'm setting it up tonight. I have it all laid out. I might even sit outside tonight, see if I get any sales, then open back up early and just lay in the sun all day, reading and trying to sell the ex's stuff at any price offered before I move. Or before we move?"

Nathan takes a deep breath, choosing not to address Ginger's question. She had tossed the idea at him a few days ago and he dismissed it, thinking she was kidding. Perhaps she is.

Ginger pauses for a beat then goes on, "He left me with so much useless stuff, Nathan. His money I can use. His stuff, not so much." She laughs absently, a deep laugh, gritty, like that of an ex-smoker. He finds it sexy. Everything about her is sexy.

"Or you could come tonight?"

"Not tonight. Eva wouldn't buy any excuse for me to leave now. Maybe tomorrow. I'll talk to you soon, baby," he says, walking back inside.

Sam runs toward him; she slides along the kitchen floor on her socks then turns and begins to slide again but here she trips and catches herself on the counter, dangerously close to the boiling pot. He gives her his stern look, and she nods. She sits in a chair and begins to doodle on a table napkin as her father listens to someone speak to him over the phone. He stirs the macaroni and pulls out Eva's veggie burger and three beef patties that he'd purchased from the deli, already portioned and ready to go. He wonders what Sam thinks, perhaps she imagines he is doing secret business on the phone, maybe that he was working toward a job. She was an optimistic girl.

"Dad?"

"What, Sam?" Nathan holds the phone with both hands, as though to conceal it.

"I'm sorry I asked for a bike." She smiles and holds up a caricature of him she'd drawn; his nose looks a piece of macaroni and his eyes are large. He has one brow arched and the other straight, and he seems to look sinister.

He likes it, gives a thumbs-up; happy, the girl takes her artwork and bounds off to the living room to show her mother.

He returns his attention to the phone. "Tell you what, maybe we'll stop by after all. I still don't know for sure."

"I heard her sweet little voice just now, Nathan. You know, I have a bike here to sell. It's big. An adult bike, an old-fashioned one that I think would be too big, but if she wants a bike bad enough…"

"Hold the bike. We'll be there tomorrow. If the bike works out, maybe I can come back later, too. Maybe we can get some dinner."

"I want more than dinner."

"Me, too."

After he clicks the phone off, Ginger remains on the line. She does not hear a dial tone, but a woman's voice. "You're taking this too far," Eva says.

"I'm helping you, Eva. I'll let him go soon, but how else can we do this? You never come over unless you need money. You still believe in that lowlife? That asshole? Let me take care of you, Eva."

"I heard you ask him to move. That is taking it too far. I have a family, Ginger. I love you, but it's two against one. And, it's different—"

"It's a penis. It's not different. He's a sorry excuse for a man. You're not happy. Move on. I'm telling you, he's thinking about my offer. Do you really want to stay with a man who'll leave you? A man stupid enough to leave you for someone who doesn't even want him? We should raise Sam together. You should be the one to come with me."

"Fuck you," Eva says, dropping the phone.

***

Eva stops at Ginger's house before work. The sun is rising as she walks up the steps and she stops to admire the angelic scene of pink and purple clouds. Ginger's light arm embraces her around the stomach. Their lips meet before anything is said, and for a moment it is as though the argument never happened. The passion spreads between their lips, opening Eva's mind to the possibility of love. It's always this way at first. Ginger is her tender place, her stability. Ginger has become everything that was missing when Nathan began to withdraw from their relationship so many months ago.

When Eva met Ginger it was in the middle of a long work day at the hotel. Eva's eyes were swollen from tears shed during another argument with Nathan. She never cried around him—she wouldn't give him this pleasure, but upon leaving it was always the same. In her car, she would sob, feeling childish and ridiculous. Sometimes the hurt would hit her later, sneak up on her and smack. This morning had been more of the same. By afternoon she felt the gamut of sadness that had been building up since she slammed the door in her husband's face that morning. Eva stood at the hotel counter wondering why Nathan didn't get a job. He had been laid off weeks ago and the bills were piling up, stressing them both. Yet, he sat at home all day rooted to the couch feeling sorry for himself.

Ginger arrived as patrons always did, when Eva was feeling badly. Her look resembled many other women who Eva checked in, but she walked leisurely, as though she had nowhere to be. She was not rushed and irritable. She wore a blue pinstriped suit and matching blue heels with small flowers at the big toe of each. She stood silently at the counter, smiling, looking Eva in the eyes when she spoke. She was patient when Eva's computer froze, causing her the inconvenience of repeating personal information. After Eva handed the woman a room key, the newly introduced Ms. Ginger Shapiro asked Eva if she had already taken her lunch for the day.

"I'd really love to have company for lunch," Ginger tempted. "I was thinking that Greek restaurant I saw down the street, if you're interested."

Eva knew she didn't have the cash to eat out and explained to Ginger that although her offer was kind, and no she had not taken her lunch yet, she would have to pass.

"My treat, please Eva," Ginger pleaded, reading her hostesses' nametag.

Ordinarily Eva would have passed, but there was something about this woman that called out against instinct.

The women ate gyros and drank beer. Eva did what she never did at this lunch: she talked about herself, her problems. She wouldn't accept a gyro, but instead picked at a plate of hummus and pita that the restaurant had brought out as an appetizer. Eva began confiding in this woman, whom she barely knew, saying that her husband was cold and unattached. She explained how much it hurt to not feel loved. Something about Ginger made Eva feel comfortable to say everything she had kept in for so long.

After listening patiently, Ginger countered her story with one of her own. It was a tale of physical abuse and neglect. After this story, Eva asked for Ginger's advice. "Nathan would never hit me, but I understand neglect. Something needs to change."

"I just divorced my husband of ten years. It took me ten years too long." Ginger said this and reached for Eva's hand. Eva did not respond to the cue. "Most men are inherently flawed when it comes to adult relationships, Eva. Please, don't be one of those weak-willed women who folds under man's brutish, clumsy weight. You may wake up one day and realize how late it is in your life, realize that time has been stolen from you and for what? Do yourself a favor and leave him."

"That's kind of harsh, don't you think. I mean we have a beautiful child, she's eight now. Besides, it's not that I don't love Nathan. It's just that Nathan isn't himself. I keep waiting for him to come back, but, well, it's hard to explain."

"I know," Ginger assured. She squeezed the top of Eva's hand as it rested on the table.

"I think I'm late," Eva said suddenly. "Thank you for lunch. I needed someone to talk to."

The women spoke again the next morning, then again that night on the phone. Ginger spent time at the hotel often, whenever her husband was in town. He was moving from their house and she didn't want to be anywhere near him. Everything between the women was subtle: Ginger's offers to help financially had begun with that lunch and eventually became offers to pay off electric bills, to pay off all bills. Eva eventually stopped accepting the handouts, feeling sick each time she did. Then, when Ginger offered to expose Nathan for what he really was, Eva couldn't resist. She wanted a reason to leave him. Ginger wanted to give her one. "I'll take care of you through him. He's my broke down vehicle, delivering my gifts, my love," Ginger had explained.

"This is getting strange," Eva said. Then, when Ginger pulled her in the first time and kissed her, Eva felt—for the first time in months—companionship, tenderness. She decided to allow Ginger to prove what she knew.

Now, Eva thinks, Ginger is everything Nathan is not and if Nathan really does decide to leave his family this would only be proof. She feels empty this day. Ginger pulls familiarly at her waist.

"Set up your garage sale," Eva says. "Prove what you've got to prove." She pulls away.

"After I sell all this, the house is next. It will happen fast. You have to chose me," Ginger called. "I'll take care of you."

**

The morning sun peers through the blinds and cuts warm lines across Nathan's face, waking him gently. Eva has already left for work. A note on the pillow beside him apologizes for the prior night. These notes are regular occurrence. They always have big and small hearts drawn all over and a kiss mark reminiscent of her lips. Sometimes this mark is maroon, sometimes pink. He decides there is a strong correlation between her bad moods and the maroon lipstick. He has planned on keeping track. He feels no tenderness as he looks over the bubbly note. He is sick of her moods, her apologizing.

It is Saturday. Eva would only work a four hour shift at the hotel. Nathan knows that he will have to make the most of his alone time with Sam. He walks to her room where she sits on the floor reading some book about teenagers that he could tell was too old for her by the seductive pout of the girl on the cover. "What do you think about going to look at a bike today?"

"A bike? You're not serious, Dad."

"It may not work for you, but there's a garage sale on Michigan Avenue, and I saw a bike there. We can go look at it, but don't get your hopes all up about it."

"Yes sir!"

Ginger sits in the sun with a steaming mug of tea and a bowl of cookies on a small foldout table next to her. She is petting the small dog whose leash extends to the hand of a stooped woman. The woman seems to be rummaging through a box of dishware as though she is looking for something she lost in there. She examines each piece briefly, checking the stamps on the bottoms, before placing it to her side. The dog jerks her hand and she drops a mug. "Oh!" she says. "Oh no!"

"Don't worry about it," Ginger says as the woman picks up the ceramic pieces.

"Oh, I'll pay you. How much?"

Ginger smiles, says, "No worries." Nathan hears her say this often, and for some reason he can't pinpoint, it bothers him.

Ginger's dark blonde hair cascades down, loosely styled, shiny. Her face is a series of perfect curves and artificial youth. When she'd first admitted her age, Nathan said he didn't believe her. He did, of course, but he knew better than to say so. She explained that there was no shame in aging, but there was no shame in her bi-monthly trips to get Botox injections either. Ginger has a small sloped nose and large round eyes. She locks Nathan into a stare and bites her bottom lip. He smiles in turn, and then turns to watch his girl in her pink t-shirt and brown shorts, bounding from one table to the next, watching the elderly woman scrutinize a crystal bowl and checking the underside of a set of bookends similarly. Sam quickly loses interest and surveys the scene for a bike, what she sees instead excites her. She runs past her father and up to Ginger. "Are the cookies free?"

Ginger nods absently, examining Sam as she holds out the plate. Nathan sees something callous to Ginger's brief interaction with his daughter. Maybe it's just his imagination. Sam rushes by the garage door and laces her arms around a shiny green bicycle that stands as tall as she is. She begins stroking it. He can tell it is not love. The bike is not like Angel's, but in the mere seconds for Sam to conclude that she has two options: bike, no bike. And, just like that, she begins jumping up and down.

"I want it, Dad."

"It's big, sweetie. You know you'll probably need a ladder to get up on that thing."

"Ha—so you know I'm growing fast, right? You always say that. So, I'll grow into the bike." She turns to Ginger, who was walking toward them with a plate of cookies. "How much is this bike, Ma'am?"

"How much you got?" Ginger teases.

"Four dollars."

Nathan scolds, "Sam, what did I tell you? You have to learn to negotiate with people, don't offer them everything you have up front."

"Three dollars, huh?" Ginger says. She holds the cookies out to Sam in the same way a person may feed a large animal, as though she doesn't want to get too close. Sam looks wary but takes a few. Trading a pleading look for the cookies.

"Ma'am, I'm sorry, it's the best I can do."

"Great negotiation," Nathan says.

Ginger takes a long moment before conceding: "It's a deal."

"Really? Wow. Thank you."

"Let's do a quality check," Nathan says, looking the bicycle over. "The chain guard looks a bit bent, maybe we can talk her down."

Ginger laughs as Sam assumes a horrified look. "Don't, Dad. Shhh. She'll change her mind." She attempts to hoist herself up on the bicycle and cannot do it. "Can you help me, Dad?"

Nathan lifts his daughter on the bike, steadies her there, and then let go. She begins pedaling fiercely, but the bike topples over to the side. "Take your time, Sam. It takes a little while to learn to ride a bicycle."

"I know how to do it, Angel taught me. Put me up there again, I'll show you."

Nathan did as he was instructed and much to his surprise, Sam was pedaling again, steadying the bicycle and riding down to the end of the driveway. "Impressive, girl."

"It's yours, Nathan," Ginger coos. "She's an, uh, a cute girl. Looks like her mother."

"What?" The smile was gone. Nathan begins to grind his teeth. "Sam, we're leaving." He throws three dollars at Ginger and turns, figuring it better if he doesn't know more. How the two women had met was something he could only guess.

"Come back, Nathan," Ginger yells.

"Dad, you know that woman? She's pretty. And she's nice, kind of weird. Is she Mom's friend?" Before getting her answers, Sam's mind continues to race. She continues to speak in a long stream of conscious as she has acquired the habit of doing. "Here, Dad, why don't you drive home and I'll ride the bike? I think I'll name it Frog, because it's green."

Nathan explains that the ride would be too long on a bicycle and that she should give herself time to get used to it. He congratulates her on her purchase, and the two head home, Sam talking the whole way, Nathan quiet.

When they arrive home with the bicycle Eva is at the table staring at her nails. "I have hard working hands, guys," she says not looking up.

"Mom, Mom, Look!"

"What on earth is that?" Her eyes widen at the bike.

"It was three dollars, Mom. We negotiated."

"You should've seen her negotiate, E, you'd be proud."

"Oh. Well, then, good for you. Negotiating is a good skill. One most women don't have." Eva smiles and hugs her daughter, giving the bicycle a once-over. "I'll take you to the park soon, baby, Okay? For now, could you do me a favor though? Could you take your bike down to the basement and let mommy and daddy talk?"

"Okay," Sam said. "I need to clean him anyhow."

"I got a phone call while you were gone." Eva starts as her daughter begins easing the large bicycle away. Nathan stares, waiting for her to finish. He is immobile. His jaw is clenched tight enough to ache. "You got called back to work. There's welding jobs an hour away at a factory in Madison County, but the bad news is that it won't be for two more months. They think this is a sure thing. They said if you can do it, to show up at this address at 7a.m. and fill out some paperwork." Her cheeks rise slightly but she does not show what Nathan would consider a full-fledged smile. She speaks softly, hesitantly.

"Are you going to go?"

"Of course, E. Of course."

"Good. We can't go on like this too much longer."

"We weren't that bad off."

"Nathan."

The two lock eyes, frozen in a single thought until a loud thump comes from the basement stairs followed by a high-pitched squeal. Eva runs, Nathan close behind her. They find their daughter crying, silently, as her mother had, blood covering the stairs she was on, covering her leg. "The bicycle cut me, Mom. I think I need to go the doctor."

"Let me see," Nathan said. He pushes beyond his wife and examines the cut. "Get me a towel, Eva." The gash is a few inches long and he can't tell how deep. "This bleeding is good for you, sweetie, you're being strong. Remember, when you bleed like this, you rid yourself of all the bad stuff."

"Don't tell her that," Eva says. She presses a towel against her daughter's leg. "Were you trying to ride the bicycle down stairs?"

Sam nodded. "No." She points to the chain guard.

* * *

Nathan watches his girl sleep, her leg covered in gauze the hospital gave them. The doctor said Sam had a minor flesh wound, that she may be a bit anemic, which would explain all the excess blood. Nathan kisses his daughter, recalling how tough she had been, how strong. "Just like you're mother," he says softly. He strokes her forehead and turns to find his wife leaning in the doorway. She follows suit, kissing her daughter's sleeping face.

"She's perfect," Nathan says.

Eva nods. "We were able to do one thing right." She leads her husband into the bedroom. He wants to say so much, to apologize and beg her to forget everything, to ask her what she knows. Does she know that Ginger has been paying the bills? That her salary hadn't even been coming close? Does she know that he still loves her? Does she know he was just doing what he had to? Does she hate him? Is she planning on leaving? Maybe she doesn't know anything. Maybe she was referring to any woman when she said, "that bitch sold you two a dangerous bicycle."

"Nathan, it was never the work that I minded." Eva says, her voice low, barely discernable. No sooner does she hear her words than she wants to take them back. She doesn't want to address the nastiness of everything, the depression between them.

"I looked that bike up," Nathan says at last. It's not for kids. It's vintage, from the sixties. I'm sorry I bought it."

"I'm sorry, too."

Silence fills the room, making it difficult for either of them to breath. The thickness of their silence comforted them for so long, kept them together and now it's time, they each think, to confront it.

"We need her help one more time, Nathan. We can't afford that doctor's visit today. We need her help one more time and then you have to stop you hear me? You'll be back to work and you'll have to stop."

"You know I never slept with her," Nathan says.

"I know."

He watches her eyes, pulling him in, offering something that he had been refusing to see. He calls Ginger, his wife lying beside him. They hold hands silently as he tells her, plainly, to never call their house again.

Mistresses never listen. The house phone rings incessantly for days, and Nathan eventually changes his cell number. Eva insists they keep the land line, in case of emergencies, and she answers each time only to then hang up; the calls don't bother her—she can wait them out.

Eva feels purged. Nathan takes a job at a gas station to supplement the welding work. He comes home and sits on the couch silently at the end of long, monotonous work days. Husband and wife listen to their daughter talk about her day; she's got an impressive scab now that she's hoping will turn into a scar that she can show off for years to come.

***

The household persists in comfortable silence, interrupted only for basic communication. Until, over dinner, Sam begins talking about the pretty woman who sold her the faulty bike. She says that the woman appeared at recess and told her that she deserved a real mommy. She asked Sam to come away with her, promising they could go anywhere she wanted. Sam recounted the story theatrically, mocking the woman whose wrists gleamed of gold and shoes spiked their way into the ground.

"She looked so full of herself. So silly," Sam says. "She said she was my mom because she had been buying my meals. She said I should listen to her and I laughed in her face. Then, and don't get mad at me, Dad, I told her to go straight to hell," like Mom said to those bill collectors that used to call. Then she left. I saw her trip on her high heels as she walked away and I laughed at her again. Angel did, too, because she heard the whole thing."

***

Eva and Nathan leave for Ginger's house while Sam is with her friend. They walk up to her door with militant strides and stern faces. They ring the doorbell, knock, and wait. "I'm going to kick her ass once and for all," Eva says.

"I'm going to watch," Nathan says. They kiss, but it's a peck, as though this kiss is a sort of test run for the real thing. "I don't think anyone lives here anymore," Nathan says.

"Come on," Eva whispers. They move around the bushes and peek inside windows. Nathan hoists his wife to the window. "It's empty," she says. "She moved."

Nathan loosens his grip and allows Eva's soft, slightly curvy body rub against his own. For the first time in months her body arouses him. He holds her hand, turning it over. Her wedding ring is tight, her hands feel rough. He kisses them. "Forgive me," he says.

Eva shrugs. "It was both of us."

They walk around to the back of the house, sitting where Ginger had been with her mug during the garage sale. Nathan recalled her long legs, a bowl of cookies by her side. The same cookies Eva had given her that morning. Ginger seemed unreal to Nathan now; perhaps he'd always felt this way. To Eva, she was merely a mistake, gone; a relief. "So, now that we have the bills paid up, why not go get our girl a real bicycle?" He asks.

"You know that girl hasn't complained about the bicycle once. She hasn't asked for anything since. She sure deserves it."

"We could get breakfast like we used to at that little place on Huebner Road? We'll get her a bicycle her size, and wrap it up for her. Then, we can go to breakfast."

"We haven't been to the place on Huebner in months." They both sit in silence. Nathan still holds his wife's hands as he imagines Sam's reaction when he tells her to get ready for the chocolate chip pancakes at the place on Huebner. He wonders if Eva will still want pancakes tomorrow; he hopes so.

A Little Taste of Heaven

The last time I saw Michael he was incarcerated, only visible behind stained, cloudy Plexiglas. His features had begun to harden after only a month's time. I wore a tight, pink shirt under my cardigan so that I could casually undress, if only a little, to provoke him. I knew that I looked irresistible that day, and this mattered to me more than anything on the outside.

It's been almost a year since the day I last saw Michael. He's thirty now. I'm twenty-two, and I'm staring at a sizable box of orthopedic shoes that I bought on the advice of a co-worker, wondering if I spent too much, when he calls to say he wants to stop by. I don't think twice. Michael is a handsome, thuggish guy, always dressed in a plain t-shirt and jeans. Always in shape, showing off his half-sleeve tattoo, an image of his brother's face with RIP scrolled below it. The image bothered me the first time we made love because Michael rested his arm on the pillow beside my head to hold himself up as he thrust—he knew how to move with me, how not to try too hard like most men—and his brother would be there, on the peak of a bicep, staring at me if I opened my eyes.

***

I'm not surprised when he's late. He's always late. An hour passes before I even call to see where he is, and when he doesn't answer, I can't lie, my heart hurts a little. I took the day off, even though Sundays mean good money at IHOP, the best shift, in fact. Now that I think about all that money I gave up, trading my shift for a Tuesday afternoon, I think I might just kick his ass. I call again. He doesn't answer.

I give up on Michael and throw away the shoe box and open a bottle of Boones Farm wine, strawberry flavor, which has been collecting dust on my kitchen counter. The wine bites just enough to balance out the syrupy sweetness. I call again. He answers—he's on his way, got caught up in something, somewhere. His voice is nice, smooth and deep, and I sink into my chair, allowing it to encase me like a thick blanket. I ask him how far away he is, and he laughs. There's a knock at my door.

Let it be known, please, that I am not the type of girl to get all wrapped up in some man, but I feel downright weak when I see Michael today. There's no cloudy wall between us. He stands a full six feet, muscular and handsome, wears a plain black t-shirt and dark jeans that are a little too big. His eyebrows are thick and dark, and he's due for a shave, which turns me on. I'm the star of my own seedy little romance novel in this moment, and I want to be ravaged by him. He looks at me with that sly grin and then pulls me in, a tight hug. "I'm finally here, beautiful girl," he whispers.

I think about schlepping greasy eggs and potatoes to unappreciative customers, some of which are still drunk at eight in the morning. I think about how a sixty dollar shift ends with tightness around my temples and sore, swollen feet. I think about how different things could be if only Michael were someone else. He sells crack, and there's no way to make a thing like that sound glamorous. Michael is in the business of selling poison to people who only want a break from life—a little taste of heaven; people who never found it in a man like him. If only he were born somewhere else, to different parents. Maybe he'd be selling for a drug company, selling the legal way and we'd be married, have a big house in Cleveland or Akron. Maybe he'd wear suits and travel on a company card, and sometimes the drugs would be good, do good, and so this would balance the effects of the addictive ones. He doesn't want to sell crack. He's told me this in letters, but it's what he knows, and he can't do what he doesn't know. How can anyone?

Our lips touch and lock, fitting together like puzzle pieces, and there's no going back. There's no going forward either, though, and I know this. I suppose I've known it for some time.

"You look upset," he says, sensing my hesitation. He grabs my shoulders and pulls back, examining my face. I try to smile but can't. I think about my sore feet, which I have stuffed into spiky heels just for him. I think about work, bills, every ordinary thing in my life, everything that keeps my days moving forward. The pink bottle is almost drained, sitting on the floor next to my chair. My orthopedic shoes, which cost me two days of tip money, are lined up beneath my apron which is hanging on the wall tree beside the door. I think about how hard I work every day and begin to cry. I cry like a mad woman, and before I know it, I'm yelling at Michael to get out and never come back. He says I'm a crazy bitch, and I tell him that's all the more reason to get the fuck out of my apartment. I never want to see him again, I yell. He slams the door.

I don't answer his calls until the next day. When he asks me if I'm okay, I tell him, no. "I want my own taste of heaven," I say. He says he's confused, but I don't care. All I can think about are my sore-ass feet, and how they better move me forward.

A Poor Mentality

The first time I met my husband was in my living room. I was running downstairs to the kitchen to get some tea while I waited for my bath to fill, and there he was relaxing on the couch as though he lived there. He was a stranger in my home, but I was accustomed to seeing strange men in my home, and I knew he must have been invited.

"I'm Jason," he said, "Alyssa let me in." There was something auspicious about his smile, and I concluded immediately that Jason was someone I'd share a beer with soon. I wanted to make a good impression, so I introduced myself and offered him some tea, which he declined. "We're heading to Rotollo's soon, and we stopped by to invite you." I could smell a mixture of smoke and some cedary cologne or aftershave as I shook his hand. I hoped he couldn't smell me; the coat of sweat I wore from my mid-day, mid-summer run. I told him that I'd be happy to join them, but I had to get ready first, and I headed back upstairs, without tea.

The three of us walked to Rotollos, a small, family-style Italian restaurant that was locally famous for its pizza and stromboli. It was early for dinner yet, and I could tell the place had just opened by the lemony scent of freshly-cleaned counters and the empty white-clothed tables, each with a small vase of silk flowers at its center. Alyssa, my tiny, curvy friend with her booming voice and loud clothes, was immediately irritated that there was no one waiting to greet us at the door. We took seats at the bar on high maroon and white stools.

We heard some rustling in the back, and a moment later a tall, slender man emerged with fringed paper place-mats and tall menus. "Welcome," he said with a tight smile.

"Are you all back there taking a smoke break or something? We've already been here for five minutes," Alyssa said. The man narrowed his eyes but his smile didn't waver.

"It hasn't been five minutes," Jason said as he reached for a menu; the way he spoke to Alyssa, without a hint of irritation, made me think he must know her well.

The server said he'd give us a few minutes to look over the menu, but when he turned, Alyssa called after him: "We have drink orders. You know, we'll probably spend more money on libations than food so you might as well start us off. I'd like a Blue Moon."

"We just started carrying the Blue Moon," he said with a slightly wider smile that made me wonder if we were the first customers to order it. "And for you?" he asked me.

"Same."

"Same all around," Jason said.

The bottles were placed before us and uncapped. Alyssa asked for some orange slices, which caught the server off-guard. He excused himself, saying he had to go get an orange.

Jason was sitting between Alyssa and me. I was yet to figure the exact nature of their relationship, but I figured they were dating because this was usually the case. She had a lot of dates, most of them being first dates. We lived near the OSU campus, even though neither of us was a student, and the proximity to a large campus meant a girl like Alyssa would never have to spend a lonely night. She had found the apartment after landing a job as a receptionist in the admissions building of the school. The job had only lasted two weeks, but during that time someone there told her about a two-bedroom townhouse for less than $500 a month. Because we were friends, and because we could both stand to save some money, we decided to live together. The neighborhood was loud, especially during football season, but we were loud, too, and so it worked. Somehow though, after four months, neither of us had managed to save any money. And although we still hung out regularly, our friendship was showing signs of strain.

"Does it really take this long to cut up an orange?" Alyssa asked me. I told her to forget about the fruit and leaned over to clink the neck of my bottle to hers. Jason lifted his, and the two of us drank.

"Kat, how many times do I have to tell you that if you let people get away with shitty service, it's the same thing as saying that you *deserve* shitty service."

When the server returned, he greeted my friend with a sincere apology. "We're out of oranges, so sorry."

"Perhaps you should've checked on that before serving the beer?" Alyssa said, pushing her bottle toward him.

I could see Jason's face redden slightly and I shoved him, extending an empathetic smile. This is just how it is with her, my smile said, and he responded with a shrug. He reached out for her beer and said, "I'll drink this one, too. What would you like instead, pretty girl?" He lifted some of her thick, amber-colored hair and then released it to fall down her back.

"A round of Girl Scout Cookies," I said. And to my delight, the man began preparing them immediately. "Impressive," I told him, standing up so that I could lean over and watch. "Most people have to ask what's in them, or look it up. What's your name?"

"Vince," he said.

"It's good to meet you, Vince." I extended my hand, noting the loose, tentative nature of his grip, his shy glance up at me before returning to his task. When our shots were ready, Jason ordered a large Mediterranean-style pizza with whole wheat crust, an order of breadsticks and an Italian sub. "What do you girls want?" he asked.

Vince assured us all that the pizza would be big enough for all of us, and despite my growling stomach telling me otherwise, I said a few pieces of pizza would be more than enough for me. Alyssa and Jason began kissing as we waited for the food and I rolled my ankles around, feeling the tightness in my calves from the run. Running was a new hobby of mine, and my legs seemed angry about it.

"Jason, my new friend," I interrupted. "Thank you for buying me dinner." Alyssa laughed.

"You date me, you date Kat. That's just how it works."

"Cheers to that," Jason said, and we all lifted our glasses. I felt the warmth of the sugary liquid expand in my throat, and then my head.

"What the hell was that?" Alyssa asked me, scrunching her perfect little slope of a nose. She made a smacking sound with her tongue then called out, "Sir! Sir, sir, can you come back out here, please?" She yelled directly into the mouth of the kitchen where Vince was undoubtedly slaving away over a hot stove, acting as server, cook and manager. I imagined him being the only one working, and my heart went out to him. He had already exhibited more patience than most did when it came to Alyssa. "Sir!" she called out again.

"His name is Vince," I said.

"Vince," she said to me, and then louder, toward the door, "Your cream is bad." She stood on the low rung of her stool so that she could bend over to see behind the bar. Her small but full cleavage pushed into the wood, and I thought about how sexy this might have looked to Jason if she wasn't acting like such a bitch.

"Leave him alone, Alyssa. You're complaining about every possible thing," I said. "Don't you ever get tired of this routine?"

"Poor mentality," she said, pointing across Jason to my forehead. "It's a shame that you, my friend, will always be poor. But don't try and drag me down with you. You can drink rancid cream all you want. Swallow it down, Kat. But you better stop trying to make me settle like you because I never will." She smacked Jason on the arm. "You know I don't settle, right? Back me up."

"I really don't see the correlation," he said breezily, leaning back to remove himself from the middle of the argument.

Alyssa went on, "If a woman, especially a woman our age, assumes a sense of entitlement, people will respect her. Unfortunates like my friend Kat here think themselves undeserving, and so they will always *be* undeserving." She turned to me. "You realize that's why John beat you, don't you? He'll end up married to some bitch like me, and he won't think of touching her."

"Over the line, girl," I said.

Jason sat up straight again and looked at me, his mouth a straight line, serious. He said, "I'm sorry. I hate assholes like that. They make all men look bad."

"He hit me once, and I left. It wasn't like I stayed with him. Fuck, Alyssa! I'm embarrassed now. Why did you have to bring that up now? You always take things too far."

"I just worry about you, girl."

"Bullshit." I stood. Vince came out with a steamy pizza topped with spinach and two kinds of cheese, including crumbles of feta, juicy pieces of tomato and generous slices of red onion. I remembered my hunger and sat down.

"Vince, did you not hear me yelling? I think your cream is bad. You should check the date on that cream."

"Ignore her, Vince."

"Shut up, Kat. Check, Vince, check it." She pointed to the small fridge below the bar. Vince crouched down to open the small door and check the carton.

"August 03rd," he said.

"So it's good for a week yet," I interjected.

"Did you leave it out in the sun after you bought it," she asked him, seriously.

"That's it, I'm out of here," I said. I pulled a five dollar bill from the back pocket of my jeans and handed it to Jason for the drinks. He pushed it back toward me as I said goodbye to Vince.

"Bye," he said and then, sweetly, waved. I looked back when I reached the door. Alyssa was eating—she was used to our fights—and Jason was watching me. I gave him a shrug, and for a moment, our eyes remained locked.

Later that night, all was forgiven. The three of us played Trivial Pursuit until Alyssa said she didn't want to play anymore and gave me a familiar look—her brows lifting, eyes angled toward my room. I pretended to not notice and so she said, "Kat!" and repeated the telling glance.

"You kids have a good night," I said. But when I got upstairs, I couldn't sleep. What's more, my stomach was growling again. After a quiet while, I tiptoed downstairs and found both Alyssa and Jason passed out in the living room. I was pleased to see them there, fully dressed and snoring on opposite sides of the room. She was on the couch; he was on the recliner by the door. I made my way into the kitchen and found an empty pizza box on the counter.

A whisper startled me. "Sorry," Jason said, walking toward me with sleepy eyes. I smiled. "I finished it off a few minutes ago. That pizza was awesome, even Alyssa wanted more."

"It's probably best it's gone," I said. I motioned to Alyssa, who was snoring, open-mouthed. "She's knocked out, eh?"

"She wore herself out," he said.

"I don't want to hear about that. Hey, you want some iced tea now? I made it yesterday. It's chai, a spicy blend." He nodded, smiling, and I poured us each a generous glass. We took our tea to the back porch, where Alyssa and I spent most nights enjoying the cool, night air.

"So how long have you known Alyssa?" I asked, pushing the porch swing back and forth with my bare toes on the gritty wood. I stopped the swing and patted the place beside me.

"A few days only."

"You seem like a nice guy. I love my friend, but I have to warn you…" What was I doing? "Nevermind."

"You have to say it now," he said, and perhaps to sound less demanding, he added, "I'd really like to know."

"Alyssa's a good friend, a good person. But, well, you know how she's always talking about entitlement, saying she has to demand what she wants?" He smiled, staring down at the porch, and I wondered if I needed to go on. He seemed to know what I was going to say. "I was just going to tell you, she's like that with boyfriends, too. She likes to get what she wants."

"So you're saying she'll use me up?" He laughed.

"It's none of my business. Let's talk about something else," I said.

"How about we discuss your new admirer?" he asked. I turned, waited. "I settled the bill at Rotollo's, and our server asked me to give this to you." He began searching his jeans for something. "I don't know where I put it. He gave me his phone number to give to you."

"Oh yeah? Vince did seem nice. Anyone who could take that much abuse…" There I was doing it again! "I mean, anyone who can keep his cool."

"I said I'd give you the number, but I seem to have lost it. Sorry. I mean, it could be in that chair, but I'm pretty sure I threw it out, along with the receipt."

"Sure of that, are you?"

"Um, yeah. You know, Alyssa is pissed at me. I think I offended her last night, after you went to bed." This news put a big, dumb smile on my face, which I tried to conceal by taking a sip of tea. The cardomom and cinnamon gave it a bite that I liked. I asked what he did.

"Her attitude is a bit much for me is all. I told her so. Then, I told her she should start meditating. Kat, your friend snapped when I said that. She actually swung at me!" Picturing Alyssa's creamy skin getting visibly warm as she swung her skinny arms at this solid-built man made me double over in laughter. I tried to stop, but I couldn't. At least, not until she appeared in front of me, just as angry as I had imagined. I laughed harder.

"Fuck you both," she screamed.

"I'll go after her," I said. "But you might want to duck out of here." Jason agreed as we stood there listening to the slams and clangs of God-knew-what inside the apartment. "Bye," I whispered, still wearing the remnant smile of stifled laughter. But as I turned, put my hand on the door handle, he spoke.

"I was lying," he said. He handed me a cocktail napkin adorned with jagged lines and a barely-legible phone number. I felt him reach out to me, a soft touch on my arm as I said goodbye.

When I walked into the apartment, ready to be a friend, I saw I wouldn't have to bother as a small, white fist struck my chin. This time, I was ready to fight.

Solitary Value

"Three days," Alice said, and everyone stopped eating. Eyes shifted toward her like slow-moving magnets. Then, more pronounced movements began; a wheelchair turned, a cane jostled across the floor, a series of slow stepping walkers made their way toward her.

Nancy was nimble; she was the first person to walk up to the table. She settled herself into a chair and waited for Alice to say something else. Nothing. A thunder of wrinkled hands collapsed upon the table and Nancy began to yell.

"I cannot believe you spoke. The Newswoman spoke. What does it mean?" Nancy tried to capture Alice's gaze and repeated, "What does 'Three days,' mean, Alice?"

In the past two years no one had heard Alice utter one word and today she spoke two. Every resident at Dunn Creek talked about it over hash and eggs this Monday morning. Everyone except for Alice, that is. Alice fiddled with her rubbery eggs. She couldn't help but thinking that if she were to speak again it would be to say that this place served despicable food. She would call Channel 6 News and tell them to do an expose on this place. Abuse of the elderly could be found in these very eggs, she imagined she would say, smiling into the camera. She let the egg jiggle on her fork as Nancy yammered away in her ear, then the thing dropped on her lap. She removed it, leaving a yellow speck.

Nancy rambled on the entire breakfast hour. She was convinced that what Alice had said was a sign that Jesus may come to visit on Thursday, which meant she had to disclose all sins today. Alice listened aptly; she wore a reporter's ear as Nancy spoke of her young adulthood, her poverty-evoked prostitution, and a short bout with an eating disorder. Alice found it all marvelously entertaining. These stories were better than a soap opera, Nancy told them passively, as though she were speaking of another person. That is, until she recounted repentance. Here, her voice lifted; Nancy was almost singing when she got to the part about how she found her religion after tripping over a sewer drain and cracking her head wide open after a night out. Jesus was the first person to visit the ER, she said. Alice wondered how long Nancy would have been a working girl had she not injured her head; then she wondered if it was even true. This could be a story Nancy had seen on television and decided to adopt as her own. She had learned a long time ago that you can't trust the verbal memoir of anyone over the age of seventy-five, despite honest intention.

Alice noticed a slightly sour smell wafting around the room. She looked up at Nancy's sagging face, watching her speak. Could the smell be coming from her? Nancy's wrinkles tempted downward more than up, suggesting there might have been some truth to her stories. But, as Alice leaned in she found the woman to be quite nicely perfumed. The smell remained. Alice felt her eyes watering as Nancy blathered on.

Alice wanted to speak, to ask where that smell was coming from, but she could not bring her words to form. More residents sat down at Alice's table, and each of them had a different idea about the meaning of three days. A good portion of residents were of the same school of thought as Nancy, flocking to Alice for advice, thinking she may be the vessel for some prophecy. Many confided in her their demons. She listened actively, nodding, until Peter relieved her from this group. Peter. Peter was a handsome white-haired man who often sat next to Alice at mealtimes. He took the seat Nancy had occupied as soon as she left.

"You look really, truly, truly lovely today, my dear Alice," he said.

Alice appreciated Peter because he called her by her name. Although it had been common knowledge that Alice had been a reporter in her younger years, it was only part of her past. Those that referred to her as The Newswoman were not allowing her the persona of mother, wife, tennis-fanatic, and book reviewer. They did not know of her dreams as a girl to travel or that she eventually settled on the idea of retiring in London. They didn't know that her plans were obliterated when she ended up raising her granddaughter, a child who was born to an irresponsible mother. They did not see the pain Alice's daughter had put her through, or the hardships she faced when trying to raise a small child late in life alongside a husband who didn't want any part of it. They didn't care who Alice was, only what she had done. Only one thing she had done—her job.

"Lovely," Peter said once more, this time with a drawl, a slow entrance to expound his conversation. He never said much, but to Alice it always felt as though he had been speaking to her for hours. Even without speech, Alice felt their conversations were always two-sided. He paid attention to her eyes.

Alice felt Peter's eyes on her now. She didn't feel as lovely as he claimed. Peter saw it though, he told her daily. He told her to appreciate the natural pink to her cheeks and her silky dark blue eyes. She was color, he said, in a sea of gray. Having not spoken in years had actually prevented many wrinkles from forming around Alice's mouth and eyes that would have otherwise told tales of her joys and sorrows.

Peter told Alice to be wary of those religious zealots, those such as Nancy who thought of her as some sort of prophet. "All they want is something to remedy their fear," he offered, speaking loudly as though he wanted to be heard by neighboring tables. "Maybe, if you can speak again...not that I'm saying you can, but if you can, maybe tell them to go away or something. Otherwise, they'll bug you all the time, thinking you may offer some alternative to death or something." He laughed at himself for a while before growing silent. "I'm not scared of death. Are you?" Alice took a bite of toast, and savored the buttery crispness on her tongue. She shook her head slightly.

"Good. You know what, Kiddo? I'm not exactly ready, but I'm not scared. I mean, death can't be much worse than this place." Alice looked around at the peeling wall paper, the windows that didn't open. She took another bite of toast. "Thanks for listening to me, lovely, lovely, Alice." Peter kissed Alice gently on her forehead and slowly moved away from her, hobbling off to his room to watch The Price Is Right with his first glass of whiskey.

Alice walked toward the common room after breakfast, a place where residents played cards and made crafts and watched a giant flat screen television that always seemed to play soap operas.

"Hi Miss Washington, how are you today?" one of the new volunteers asked. She was a lanky girl who always wore bejeweled clips in her hair and always offered Alice a wide smile. Alice found the volunteers patronizing, so she looked away. They all spoke to her as though she were a child. "Enjoying your program today?" the girl pressed on. Alice did not look away from the screen. The girl then motioned toward the television and then leaned down to whisper, "You

know, I think Alexandra is going to come back to life any day now."
Alice thought so too.

***

Mona, one of the oldest residents at ninety-seven walked up and said, "I know you fake this. You just do this so you'll get all the attention when you feel like it. Hell, I could go mute, too, if I wanted, but now you've already done it, so no one would care. You make me sick!" Alice was in the habit of ignoring the sharp-tongued old woman, but today Mona seems violent; she begins yelling, "Speak! Just tell me why you do this! Speak!" The girl with the jeweled hair clip asked Mona to leave Alice alone. Alice noticed the same smell as before. She pinched her nose.

***

"Three days," Alice had said. She thought now, back to her anonymity before uttering these two words. The silence that she felt throughout her stay at the residence had been a welcome one, but there was appeal to celebrity, too. Maybe Mona was right. Maybe she had subconsciously concocted the whole muted persona only to shock and amaze on Monday, January 14th.

Alice wondered what to do next. Could she speak again? She had enjoyed the stories she heard and wanted them to continue. They reminded her of her work, interviewing people was always best when you gave long silences, uncomfortable ones even, to keep them blathering on. But what really consumed Alice now was what she had meant by saying it. "Three days." Three days?

Could the outside world eventually decode what she had been thinking when the words had escaped mindlessly? Or had they already decoded her thoughts? Alice contemplated the possibility that her words had meant more than what she was thinking at the time. It had been three days since she had last showered and changed. She had said this aloud, so as not to forget to change clothes when she got back to the room but no one had noticed. Consequently, Alice's thoughts were infiltrated by stories of woe, accusations of conspiracy, and now she was disillusioned by it all. She would ultimately forget again, only to wear the same blue slacks with a yellow dot and that same pink blouse on Tuesday. That is, until she would remember and say aloud, "Shit!" The entire place would be abuzz with speculation.

Jim

He comes to see me on Saturdays, after his run. We share the shower, and I breathe in the thick steam slowly as we move together. I do not leave my apartment for a while after because I like to keep his smell on me: my own Dove soap mixed with his salty self, perhaps a trace of his wife's sharp perfume. I taste the creaminess of his shoulders. He says he loves my freckles, my lips, my pale hair, especially when I let my bangs grow long enough to get in my eyes. He tousles the waves that flow down my back while I think of her; her short hair, slick and dark. I think of her full cheeks and supple curves. I want her to know, but she will not care. She would handle it, stop it.

Each day, I make small talk when she buys her cigarettes. I ask her for a discount card that will not provide her a discount. Today she tells me she's planning to quit. It drives my husband crazy, she says. I press my tongue to the roof of my mouth and a swell of air fills my throat. I tell myself it is a feeling of anger at her, but this is untrue.

He'd prefer to have me, he says. He complains of her smoking, her bossiness. Why can't she just quit, he asks me. I did. I mean, it's easy really. You just have to decide to do it. I read somewhere that it is more difficult for women, but I do not tell him this. Instead, I tell him not to give her such a hard time. She'll quit, I say, just give her time.

"I'm getting tired," he says. "Bye, Jim." She must be there, close enough that he can smell her, a mixture of smoke and over-priced perfume. I am his running partner to her, a man named Jim whom she'll never meet and never bother to remember later. I am the one who is tired, but when I close my eyes, the whole affair is picturesque. I imagine her, offering her body wholly, more completely than I ever will. Her body, lending itself to a child, sealing their deal tighter; me, finding out when she stops buying cigarettes and asks about the forty dollar gum we keep behind the counter. When this day comes, I'll quit, go back to school. When he stops running, calling, I'll do something for me. I will be content then and offer my best wishes. I will.

To the Curb

I don't want to hear another word about applications. I'm thinking I'd like to throw Ray's iPhone out the car window when I see his hands go up in front of him and the phone drop. He yells, "Watch it!"

I look up to see a figure moving slowly, only a few paces from the front of the car. I push the break hard enough that the momentum thrusts me forward and my seat belt tightens against my chest. My body becomes putty, and as the car stops I'm jerked upright then forward again to the tune of tires scraping asphalt. The blurry figure is now an inch from the bumper, and as I regain my breath his image solidifies. The man is erect, unscathed and, apparently, unaware of—or maybe unconcerned with—our near-collision. I am thankful for a few seconds, before the heat of recognition builds in my chest.

My husband and I are quiet as we watch him shuffle along. His name is Matthew, and he is a former neighbor of ours. It takes every bit of restraint I can muster to not yell out, to not get out of the car and chase him down, tell him what an asshole he is for walking out like that without looking in the middle of a busy intersection. Matthew's hair is longer than I remember and his brown curls are matted in places at the back of his head. His hunting jacket is sun-faded and his khakis are too long, street-stained and dragging on the ground behind his heels.

"It's okay. He's okay," Ray says, placing his large hand on my shoulder.

I hear a horn sound behind me, but I cannot yet move, so I direct my middle finger at the rearview. Matthew is moving as though he has an extra fifty years behind him, an extra fifty pounds weighing him down. He moves as though he's underwater, going against the current. I hit the wheel with the palm of my hand, hard enough to cause a sting and shake off my husband's hand. "Are you okay?" Ray asks.

"Stop saying okay. No, I'm not okay. I almost hit him, and he doesn't even care."

Ray bends down and searches the floor mat with the palm of his hand. "Well, you didn't hit him. Just try and calm down," he says, his voice muffled now. He feels around the seat and underneath it. My husband has gained twenty pounds since our move to Arkansas, and his movements are awkward as he shifts around the seat. His elbow is pushing against me, and I push back.

"You know what, Winnie?" he says, pulling himself upright and turning to look behind the seat. "I'm impressed. I swear, if it had been anyone else driving, that man would've been a grease spot. Good reflexes." My husband is trying to calm me down, but I can see he is frantic to find his phone.

"Sit up. I see it," I say, and angle my arm between our seats. This is my chance to throw the phone away, but we're still at a stop and he'd only go after it. So instead of throwing it, I drop it in his lap. He smiles, clutches it tightly like a child might his favorite toy and stares out at Matthew—who is almost to the curb at last. "Can you believe that? You know, Matthew wouldn't care if he were a grease spot. And don't look at him like that, Ray. He can sense it. He'll come up to us and ask for something."

Ray places his hand on my cheek as more impatient drivers begin to sound off behind us. "You're full of shit, Winnie," he says, and he turns back toward Matthew. "Are you okay?"

Matthew doesn't turn around, and as I watch Ray watch Matthew, I can only imagine what he's thinking. My husband stares helplessly the way he did weeks ago, when our bulldog was sick. As I paced that day, on the phone with the vet, I noticed my husband's worried face—the lines that normally mark his forehead were smoothed and his lips pursed tightly below his well-trimmed mustache. He stroked Henry's ears, squeezing them softly at the tips—a pressure point that, we'd read, was supposed to induce calm. Then, his compassion was admirable, but now it was ridiculous.

Matthew doesn't so much walk as wander, slowly, as though the street below heads in many direction and he's unsure which way is forward. I notice how much weight he's lost and it sickens me. He's almost to the curb and, thankfully, he hasn't acknowledged us. I push down on the gas pedal slowly and my Honda wavers a little before moving forward. "So, you think I'm full of shit?"

"Just drive, Winnie," he says and begins fiddling with his phone again, making sure it still works.

When Ray and I are angry, there is silence between us. It isn't an uncomfortable silence, but more of a silence that settles and grows slowly, creating a new space for us, a space we have been visiting more often, with more familiarity, more ease.

Before we moved to Arkansas, Ray and I fought, in a more proactive way, that is. We'd argue and sometimes, we'd yell, scream, wear ourselves out with words, only to then talk it out. I remember fighting with him over the stupidest shit. We would be driving around, looking for a restaurant and he would ask me where I want to eat. I would point out a place that looked interesting and he would say nah, he wasn't in the mood for Italian. "What do you want," I'd ask, and he'd say it didn't matter. "How about that place?" I'd ask, pointing to a small blue building. He'd say he wasn't in the mood for Greek, either. "What are you in the mood for, Ray?" I'd ask, the annoyance building in my tone, and he'd say it didn't matter. This sort of situation was not common, exactly, but it happened, and it always led to a fight. But then, I couldn't have imagined forgetting the whole thing before I even addressed it, cutting my feelings off before they had the chance to develop. Back then, I used to wish we wouldn't fight, but I couldn't hold back, and the truth was, I would sometimes enjoy the argument. I liked hearing my husband's voice deepen with resolve as his position solidified with the argument. We are both stubborn, but we would exhaust ourselves eventually. We'd argue with passion, make up with passion. And now, it seems, I don't have the energy, and so I keep quiet. No wasted tears or lengthy conversations and concessions. It's not worth it anymore.

Today is different. I let the car speak for me as I slam on the gas, turn the car sharply into our apartment complex, and shove into a parking spot with a fast break.

"What the hell is wrong with you?" Ray asks, evacuating the car as though it were on fire.

"I'm sick of this neighborhood," I say. The vague comment sounds childlike, unreasonable, even to me.

"Winnie, you're too hard on that guy. It's not like he was trying to get hit. He's sick."

"I'm not just talking about Matthew. But since you bring him up—I can't believe you're not mad at him. He could have killed us all. He's a dick."

"He didn't mean it."

"Ray, he's not a stupid man."

"He's homeless."

"You can be homeless and still be a good person. You can be sick and at least try to get better. That man is a leech, and he's destructive."

"That's unfair."

"Unfair? Have you seen his camp, Ray? The woods behind our apartment are filled with trash. He destroys himself and everything around him. He suffers; he wants the world to suffer. I gave him a few dollars once. Did you know that?"

"So?"

"So, he didn't even say thank you. All he said was 'God bless' as though God wanted him to have that money. There are plenty of people in need, especially here, and I feel bad that I gave him those dollars. I could've given them to someone who's trying, who cares, who takes responsibility and I could've kept those dollars. Hell, I still don't have a real job." My husband pulls his hand away, as though he's disgusted by me. "I'm not being mean, Ray."

"He's sick. The man is sick," Ray says, fiddling with his phone again. I feel my stomach tighten, and as my husband's voice lower, I savor the adrenaline.

***

Matthew was the first person I met in Arkansas. Then, he was in his late thirties, teenage-thin and clean-shaven. He ran over to Ray as we hauled the last of our belongings from our car. He introduced himself and asked if he could help us carry any of our boxes. Ray declined politely, so our new neighbor hovered, making polite small talk, disclosing a little more personal information than I prefer on a first meeting, but I was too tired then to think much of it. After shaking Matthew's hand and introducing myself properly, I told both men that I was going inside, to rest a while before we started unpacking. "Rest is an important thing," Matthew said. "Want to take a break yourself, have a beer?" he asked my then-fiancé, who looked at me with wide brown eyes. I kissed Ray and excused myself to the futon, the one piece of furniture we'd put together. I left the screen door open to the porch, savoring a slight breeze and resting to the sound of the men's deep voices. They were chatting about football, then spirituality, then who knows?

My nap lasted until the men had finished a six pack, and when Ray woke me up, all we had the energy for was a brief exchange about the smallness of the apartment. "It seemed bigger online, and the dimensions are right. Maybe the ceilings are just low. I'm sorry, Baby," he said. "This isn't what I expected."

Ray asked me to hold the tape measure at the base of the front door as he extended it down the hall. I told him not to bother, that it wasn't much smaller than our last apartment. "Besides, I can live anywhere a year."

Hardy, Arkansas was a temporary stop, we agreed, as we inspected the cement brick walls and stand-only shower the next morning. Our new address was 103 Perry Street, Apartment B, but soon we began referring to it as cellblock B. Matthew lived in apartment A, in the building opposite ours and was, we soon found out, always home. "He lives with his mother, but he's not too fond of her," Ray told me.

Two days after we'd moved into our new apartment, I landed a job interview at a bank. On my way to the interview, I found the driver's side window of my car shattered, and the door itself ajar as though someone had tried to pry it open first and then got exhausted and just punched in the glass. Only my radio was missing. But, because I was headed to a job interview when I found the crime scene, I admit, I probably overreacted. I kicked and cursed the ground, telling myself that they'd never hire me now because I'd be late to the interview. I was still pacing, fuming, when my neighbor arrived. Matthew told me to calm down. He said it probably happened for a reason.

"You never know. Maybe, if you would've driven that car this morning, you would've gotten in an accident. So, you see, God might've saved your life by allowing someone to break into your little Honda."

"If it happened for a reason, fine. But it still sucks," I sulked. After I called the police and my insurance company; after I called Ray and couldn't get a hold of him. "Raymond is in a meeting until one," a nasally voice said, Matthew waited with me on the steps that led down to the parking lot. He was drinking Natural Ice—the same silver and blue cans I'd seen scattered around the lot behind the apartments. He emptied two cans while we sat there. When a police officer, balding and preoccupied, finally arrived, he told me that there was nothing to be done and that whoever took off with my radio was probably long gone, but that I'd be wise to check local pawn shops where my property would likely turn up. Depleted of anger, I told myself just that once that maybe Matthew was right, maybe I wasn't meant to have the job, after all. The manager I was scheduled to interview with seemed to agree when I showed up late— our talk was less than ten minutes long, and I never heard back.

Later that day, Matthew and I played chess on my porch. We chatted about crime in the neighborhood, which he said had been getting bad. He blamed hurricane Katrina, the misplaced residents from Louisiana, who ended up homeless, squatters. "Or maybe it's these little gang bangers around here. Maybe it's some sort of initiation, to break into a car." I nodded along to all of his theories, but my thoughts were centered on the game. I took his second pawn and he stood up and said, "If I ever see someone around your car again, neighbor, I'll shoot him with my bb gun." I laughed, but he didn't join in. "And I don't have a job yet, so I can watch pretty much all day long. Really, whoever did it was lucky I didn't see them this morning."

"Thanks, Matthew. I mean, I don't want you to shoot anyone, but if you could watch that'd be great."

"Of course," he said and took a few steps back. I asked him where he was going; we were in the middle of a game! "I have to get back home before Mom gets off work. She'll have a fit if the dishes aren't done. She'll have a fit anyway, but I better get home." He looked around as though she might appear. Perhaps she had.

"I'll save the game for us, Matthew," I said. He was distracted, not listening to me.

"Hey, and Matthew, um, on second thought, go ahead and shoot the kids if you see them breaking into another car." I was joking again, trying to get his attention, and to emphasize this, I gave Matthew my biggest cheesy smile. He nodded as though he'd just been offended, or maybe he nodded as though he were taking my direction. He hurried away.

I never saw the woman that Matthew referred to as his mother, but she haunted all of our conversations. He always referred to her as "misguided," and ultimately, when he began saying she was evil, I told him to stop coming around our apartment. The worse the woman became to his mind, the more I saw him outside, drinking on the stoop, the more he asked for a few dollars here, a ride there, and the more I said no. Soon, he only came begging at our apartment when Ray was alone. The last time we spoke, he arrived at our door and before I could tell him to leave he said that his mother had forgotten to pay the rent, that they'd been evicted, and that it had been her fault. He didn't ask if he could have money this time; he simply asked for oil. He said he needed it for his lantern, to read his Bible at night. He'd been so matter-of-fact about it, as though he were asking to borrow some butter or a cup of sugar, that I gave him a cup. I gave him a few dollars.

**

Ray slams the door to our apartment.

"What am I supposed to do?" I ask, catching my voice before it breaks.

"Sorry, Baby. I really have to get this project started. Maybe you could play with Henry, take him to the park or on a walk?" Henry's ears perk at the sound of the word walk, and I grab his leash.

"Ray, I want to talk about this. I want to yell."

"Seriously, Honey, work," he says, pointing to his phone without looking up.

"Asshole," I yell. I yell it again. Ray gives me no response, not even a nod or sigh. I want his voice to lower, to see the heat rise on his face, the stubborn nature that I used to love and spar with so freely to show, just show. The space between us widens and as Henry nudges my leg with his moist nose, I say, "Fine. I'll go on a walk; that just sounds like it'll solve all my problems. In fact, I don't know what the fuck I'd do without you, Ray. You and your wonderful suggestions." I slam the door.

Of course I see Matthew as I walk my dog. Of course his ragged green coat catches my eye, and although I do my best to ignore him, to look down at the road as we pass each other, the same way he did when he passed in front of my car. The last time he spoke to me, we'd argued. He told me his mother was a bitch, for leaving him and that all rich people were evil. I told him that he was full of shit, the same way my husband, apparently, thinks I am. He smiles at me today, for the first time in a year.

To my own surprise, I, too, smile. "Long time, Matthew."

"Yeah."

"Are you still looking for work?" I ask. "We're um, hiring at the gas station."

"I can't get hired there. No one wants to hire me. Life is ... well, I guess not for you, but for me..."

I imagine myself going to prison for assaulting a homeless man. I imagine planting my fist directly into his eye socket. I imagine this, but my fury is disingenuous and I feel myself exposed as the momentum of the feelings works up to my eyes. "Come on, Henry, let's go." I tug the pup, who is busy squatting near a bush. "We're hiring at the gas station," I say again, to distract the man from the tears forming in my eyes. "They refuse to hire anyone full-time, so they're always looking for part-timers." Matthew watches me, doesn't listen.

The swell of tears pushing at my sinuses almost hurt, and I stare back. Why am I so bothered by this man? Matthew tugs at his sleeves, moves his gaze toward a group of teenagers huddled together across the street, laughing at some inside joke. Matthew pulls out a silver can and crouches down on the step of the insurance company on Windridge Road, near the very spot I almost creamed him. It's Sunday evening and the building is empty. He pats the cement step above him and I sit. I tell Henry to sit, too, which he does without hesitation. I wipe my eyes. "Winnie, right" Matthew asks, trying my name out on his lips, as though it were a flavor he wanted to savor.

"That's right," I say, and we sit for a while, just watching the group of teenagers as they laugh at one another in a mocking, competitive way, until at last they break into pairs and walk off in opposite directions.

Ray appears, my tall, serious husband, walking briskly, head darting this way and that, iPhone in hand. I call out to him and he rushes over without a word. The three of us take turns petting Henry as we sit in our silent space, and I tell Matthew that the reason the dog is shaking is because he's nervous, that the vet had recommended anti-anxiety medication, something called "Composure Serum," which makes Matthew laugh.

"I could use some of that myself," he says.

"Me, too."

Ray stands suddenly. "You coming home or what, Baby?" he asks. I shrug. Ray mentions his project again, he has work.

"I'm coming," I say. I place my hand on Matthew's flaccid shoulder before saying goodbye. As my husband walks off ahead — as though he's already forgotten he'd come here to find me, to make sure I wasn't mad — I give the shoulder a tight squeeze.

"Bye, Winnie," Matthew says. I smile; I try to see the sickness in his eyes, but they are just tired, I think, and this I can understand.

I take my time walking home, collecting my thoughts, acknowledging these last few minutes of silence.

Dandelion Ghosts

There was nothing beautiful about dandelions. They stained my skin yellow and had a musty, cheesy smell so opposite the soft scent of other flowers. The dandelion plant consumed my early Saturday mornings then, throughout the summer that I turned nine and my chore list expanded to include weeding the yard. The sun drenched my shoulders those early mornings as I muttered to myself about the injustice of my workload as it compared to my sister's.

An hour into the task, and I would still be at it, going to war with the ferocious weeds. Oddly, I thought at the time, my efforts seemed only to speed the plant's evolution. Each flower seemed to grow back stronger and more resistant each week, and I never understood why we couldn't just spray the things with chemicals and be done with it.

***

When my father and I speak on the phone, it's to reminisce. I rarely see him, since I took a job in Texas, but our distance has worked to strengthen the depth and honesty of our conversations—this, I hear, is often the case with small families. When I inquire about the purpose of those childhood lawn care assignments, my father responds without hesitation.

"I wanted you kids to develop a strong work ethic," he says.

"But," I want to say, "I would stay out there for hours." And then I remember that I'm thirty years old now, and I should probably get over it.

Dad asks me how Laura is doing, if she's working full-time yet, and I tell him that she's looking. He says he isn't going to call her no matter what. It's his new experiment; he wants to see how long she will go before reaching out, asking how he is.

When I was nine, pulling weeds in the yard, I rarely tried an excuse to get out of the job. My sister, on the other hand, would throw a fit and get her way; inevitably, she'd end up with one of the easy chores: crushing soda cans or washing dishes. At the time, I envied her resolve.

"Did you think I lacked discipline as a child?" I ask my father.

"No, Honey. I just wanted to ensure that you knew how to work. That's why I gave you big tasks, real work. The funny thing is, I never said you had to stay out there in the yard as long as you did. You would just stay out there until you were finished." He laughs then adds, "For hours!"

I tell Dad I'll call my sister when we hang up; that I'll tell her to call him. "Nah. She'll come around," he says, "in her own time." I ask him if he would've called me had I not called him first. He says he hadn't thought about it.

I'm surprised when Laura answers the phone on the first ring. I ask her how she's been, and she says not good. She lost her job, wishes she had enough money to pay her gas bill, wishes there were more job opportunities in Ohio. I draw exaggerated loops as I sign my name, making out a check she didn't ask for.

When I hang up, I begin thinking about that summers I spent crouched down in a bed of dandelion weeds. Why did I fight the weeds while my sister fought our father? And did my willingness to complete such tasks cause her to swing in the opposite direction? I think so. I decide not. And then I tear up the check before I breakdown like a smoker trying to quit. I sign my name again, reignite the small blue flame; this will be the last time.

That summer, when I was finished weeding, my sister often joined me in cursing the dandelions. We delighted in snapping the yellow heads of the weeds, and then we reached down to collect the heads and throw them into our alley where they belonged. They would settle there, along the curb with gum wrappers and cigarette butts.

At the time, we thought the yellow flowers were trash, but the white ones, which we called dandelion ghosts, were different because they granted wishes. The ghosts, we held close to our faces, cupping our hands around them as we closed our eyes. We blew the soft, cottony pedals into the air along with our secret and not-so-secret desires. Dad would tell us to stop if he saw us doing this, so if we heard him at the backdoor we'd grab handfuls of ghosts and take off running toward a nearby park, the seeds falling at our feet. The ghosts, it seemed, were never in the same patches as the yellow flowers I so despised, and so my sister and I delighted in collecting them, trying to get as many wishes as we could. I pulled a lot of weeds that summer, but I also made a lot of wishes. I tear up another check and make a wish.

***

Three months pass before I speak to my sister again. I have returned to Ohio for a short visit, and I'm nervous about speaking with her. When I call, however, she says she can't wait to see me.

I pick Laura up from her new job, which, she says, might offer her full-time hours soon. She's doing well, and she's on speaking terms with our father—who has since moved to Massachusetts. I can't help but to think about the correlation between physical distance and emotional closeness in our family, but I do not bring it up. We walk the old neighborhood, toward our childhood home.

"You look tired, Jen. You're working too much," Laura says. I see her lips purse slightly, the genuine concern, and I nod.

There is a heavy, cool breeze, the sort that comes before a light rain, and it fits with the melancholy sweetness of home. We sneak around the house, which seems paler than it was when we lived there; the trim is pastel green now. I can't remember what it used to be: something brighter, maybe blue. We sit on the back porch and peer into the backyard until we are startled from behind.

"Excuse me," a man says, stepping onto the still-creaky porch. "Can I help you?" The man's voice is soft. He doesn't sound bothered by the squatters in his backyard, just confused.

"Um, no. We're leaving," I say, but I do not explain our reason for being on his property. Laura and I exchange a look as though we've just been caught doing something wrong. We begin to laugh as we duck into the alley and take off running, just like children.

Disengaged

The closest I've come to a passionate encounter in the last two decades was with Henry, and he died soon after we met. The men I love die and, even if they live, my daily rituals are becoming too all-consuming for me to entertain distracting and emotive pastimes such as romance. I must learn to be methodical if I want to continue to live a productive life. After all, I have been elected for this self-study of old age and I should make the most of it. Take, for instance, the curious nature of my own bones as they begin to shrink and curve toward the ground. I had never really noticed my body beginning to hunch over until I got out of bed a year ago, stood up straight and realized that I was still facing the floor. The experience caused me to pay attention to the drastic changes occurring in my body each day. Sometimes I feel honored; it is as though I have been allowed the exclusive experience of old age and I should make the most of it.

I'm no cynic. I still believe that romance exists for other women as it did for my previous selves: the dreamy beauty I was in college; the first female chair of environmental microbiology, who found herself surrounded by intelligent, successful suitors; the devoted, experimental wife, ready to take on the world with my research partner and husband for more than two dozen succeeding years. But now, at eighty-six, I have been a widow for some time, and I do not mind my solitary lifestyle, the fact that romance only exists in my imagination.

Each morning, I read the latest edition of Microbe magazine or work my crossword puzzles and drink instant coffee with cream. I sit by the window and there he is again, invading my thoughts, this man I hardly know. Our single date has become my morning mediation, my visual mantra. We had not been involved sexually—the logistics of such an encounter would not have worked, what with his bad stomach and my chest pains—but we did become involved.

We were introduced by Desiree, a young woman with a full face who assisted me with housework. She was in love at the time, soon to be married to a charming business man whom she had been dating for less than a year. She got it in her head that because she was romantically involved, the elderly woman she assisted should be too. Silly girl. She would not listen to my rational reasons for staying alone. My mind, I said, was cluttered with reality and burdened by the ailing body attached to it. She said my mind was simply closed and perhaps if I would open it, I could allow for greater things.

Her clouded perception was endearing, but rather annoying. As I worked the Sunday crossword that day, I explained to her that romance is the intimacy of shared sensation, soft music and soft movement, and that there is no room in a romantic scene for the crippling effects of aging.

"Irene, I know this man named Henry who'd be perfect for you," she said. He was an uncle of her husband, a real catch.

"These crosswords are too easy these days," I said, trying to change the subject, but this girl was persistent. Ultimately, I only accepted her offer because I thought it would make her happy.

***

We met at a coffee shop that smelled curiously of lemons and vanilla. I walked in ten minutes late, thanks to an inept cabby. Henry must have known it was me: one geriatric heading toward another in a room full of college-aged kids. He began to stand, but something stopped him half-way.

"Henry," he said, extending his hand from his stooped position. I noticed that he was shaped like a bowling pin, bloated around the middle, the hips. He was not a bad looking man, not particularly handsome, but I wondered why he couldn't bring himself to stand. He looked down at his lap as he sat down again and clumsily handed me two sunflowers with long, straight stems that seemed as sturdy as tree trunks.

I thought I'd excuse myself politely, head back to the front of the coffee shop, and ask the barista to call me a cab. I thought this, but I stayed because my body craved stillness. I felt wrapped in a blanket of silence, however, and I struggled to find something to say. This burden often falls on women, and I have never had the gift for gab.

"Cappuccino," I ordered. Henry asked for more water. I searched his milky brown eyes as he stared beyond me, at a painting of a young bloodied hand that I, too, had noticed on the way in. The hand was reaching out, as though to shake or accept something and I immediately began to think of the various air born bacteria that could enter such an open wound.

"That painting makes no sense," Henry said. I hadn't thought about the artist's intentions, but I agreed. Then there was another extended silence in which I adjusted my seat and the wood scraping against the linoleum seemed to echo throughout the room.

"You're a nice man, Henry, but this date is ridiculous. I feel sixteen again, only old." I laughed at myself and adjusted a napkin.

He smiled—a fine set of teeth. I was tempted to ask him if he has a bridge or full dentures and how much they cost. "Sixteen was wretched," he said. His soft brown skin creased around the corners of his mouth as he stopped short of smiling.

We sat. I reached for a half-completed crossword puzzle beside him.

"Three down is sanguine; too short for optimistic.

"I hadn't read that one yet," he said defensively. "I don't go in order."

"You should."

"Why? Why add rules to a pastime?"

I liked his defiant energy.

"Rules are what keep us old people alive, buddy," I said. "Rules and routine." I offered him a sip of my cappuccino when it came, hoping to feed his energy, but he refused. We were silent again, but somehow it was nice. Henry never told me that he was feeling ill that day, nor did he tell me that he had digestive disorders and that one sip of acidic coffee might cause him insatiable pain for the rest of the day. We exchanged phone numbers, both planning to call each other when we found the answer. He was the first to call, an hour after I returned home. I was pleased by this.

We spoke on the telephone a few more times before he died, usually discussing the Sunday crossword, if either of us was stuck. I was never stuck, so I had to pretend. We began to crave each other's company, but I cannot honestly say we felt romantically inclined, at least I didn't. I told Desiree that she was right, I did like Henry. But I also told her that I, too, was correct. Such fables were gone from my life, retired to memory and imagination.

***

Today, I work a crossword book that promises to be tough, but alas, it disappoints. I have two pressed sunflowers on my windowsill, next to my reading chair. I often relive my date with Henry because I didn't feel the urgency around him that I feel around most people. I didn't feel as though I was a burden or that I was walking too slowly, slowing everyone else down. Desiree's marriage was annulled shortly after it was announced, after she caught the charming business man with another woman. I tell her she's young, not to give up, but I recognize the slight of my own hypocrisy. I tell her that I think of Henry often, that I just never wanted to admit our connection. I move the pressed flowers into my crossword dictionary, where I will not lose them.

Sometimes I use white-out on my favorite puzzles and have another go at them, but I remember each answer. The new puzzles baffle me now, but this vocabulary hasn't faltered; it seems it never will. I forget a lot each day: keys, pills, my purse, a jacket on a cold day; but I don't forget the answers to those puzzles. I place the completed puzzles in the window next to my crossword dictionary. This is where I keep the crispy, dried yellow petals that once lived in Henry's full lap, and I open the book to gaze at them.

***

It's been six years since I've heard from Henry, and I can't figure out why. I remember his brown eyes peeking out from between wrinkled patches of skin. I remember his silly word choices and how we could sit in silence, even on the phone, but when we spoke there was always passion. He was full of a certain energy the old men at this residency don't have. I wonder if he knows I'm here.

When Desiree comes to visit me, I notice how gray her hair is around the temples. I ask why Henry hasn't called and she tells me he's gone. She says it was pneumonia, and I think about his wounded hand, the way it invited streptococcus, a killer for men his age.

"He never complained about it, even though it looked awful. Men around here always complain," I tell her. I am ninety-two years old, and even the thought of Henry still makes me feel as though I am sixteen. He makes me feel the fluttering in my stomach that I used to think a clichéd exaggeration.

Desiree smiles and crouches down to meet my eyes with her own. She tells me she'll bring my lunch up to my room for me; that I should rest.

An herb capable of retrieving a lost love. My crossword dictionary is necessary only today. When I open the thing a yellowish dust falls onto my lap. Anacampserote is the answer I do not find. The dust shimmers against the window light, against my pale hands. I try to get out of my chair and gravity pulls me forward, reminds me of the way I am slowly shrinking, surrendering my space. Henry was doing the chivalrous thing by reminding me, in his quiet way, what love was supposed to be, and I rub the gritty powder against my skin like lotion so that my skin shimmers as I sit, waiting for Desiree, my lasagna, help to stand.

About the Author

Jen Knox is the author of *Musical Chairs*, a memoir. Jen earned her MFA from Bennington's Writing Seminars. She is the Workshop Coordinator at *Our Stories Literary Journal*, and she currently teaches creative writing at San Antonio Community College. For updates on Jen's current projects, go to http://www.jenknox.com.

ALL THINGS THAT MATTER PRESS ™

FOR MORE INFORMATION ON TITLES AVAILABLE FROM
ALL THINGS THAT MATTER PRESS, GO TO
http://allthingsthatmatterpress.com
or contact us at
allthingsthatmatterpress@gmail.com